Countdown to Mother's Day

Dianna Houx

Reading Order

1.) Countdown to Christmas
2.) Countdown to Valentine's Day
3.) Countdown to Easter
4.) Countdown to Mother's Day
5.) Countdown to 4th of July!
6.) Countdown to Halloween!
7.) Countdown to Thanksgiving!
8.) Countdown to Christmas Eve!
9.) Countdown to New Beginnings
10.) Countdown to a Wedding

I recommend reading the books in order. There is an overarching storyline that starts in book 1 and continues throughout the series. Plus, it's more fun that way!

Contents

1. Days till Mother's Day
-Ten-   1

2. Days till Mother's Day
-Nine   11

3. Days till Mother's Day
-Eight-   21

4. Days till Mother's Day
-Seven-   31

5. Days till Mother's Day
-Six-   41

6. Days till Mother's Day
-Five-   51

7. Days till Mother's Day
-Four-   63

8. Days till Mother's Day
-Three-   73

9. Days till Mother's Day   83
-Two-

10. Days till Mother's Day   93
-One-

11. Happy Mother's Day!   105

12. The Day After   117

Afterword   127

About the Author   129

Days till Mother's Day

-Ten-

T he sun was starting to rise when Grace finished her chores out at the ranch. In the four months she had been helping out, she had established a routine that coincidentally got more efficient the higher the outside temperature. The smell of horse poop was no joke, even at five-thirty in the morning.

She was about to find Cole when she spotted his ex-wife, Valerie, coming up the drive. As per usual, she was dressed like she was heading to a nightclub, not a farm. But that was Valerie for you. "What can I do for you?" Grace asked with a fake smile.

Valerie looked her up and down, her face contorting in disgust at Grace's dirt-covered (she hoped it was dirt) jeans and old t-shirt. "Why he would ever want...that," she pointed at Grace, "when he can have...this," she said, pointing to herself, "is beyond my comprehension."

Grace rolled her eyes; this was not the first, nor even the third time, she had heard Valerie utter those words. "Cole is a rancher," Grace said patiently, as if addressing a toddler. "He prefers me because he wants a partner, not a trophy wife. You weren't happy here the first time, Valerie. And since you haven't changed," Grace eyed her up and down, "why do you think you'll be happy now?"

"Not that it's any of your business," she huffed. "But Cole was my first love. The one that got away. I know that now, and I am determined to right the wrong that was done to us."

"Wow," Grace said with a snort. "You are far more delusional than I thought. Nothing was done to you, Valerie; you did it all yourself when you decided to cheat on Cole and leave him for another man."

"I was a different person back then," she said defensively. "And so was Cole. He had just inherited this place, was always working, and was broke. Things are different now."

"By 'things,' you mean he's no longer broke," Grace stated as she rolled her eyes for the second time. She crossed her arms over her chest and shook her head.

Valerie stepped forward and pointed her finger at Grace. "Now, see here, you have no right to judge me. Just because you're happy rolling around in horse poop while dressed like a hobo doesn't mean I have to be. A woman is allowed to have needs, and my needs cost money. There's nothing wrong with wanting the finer things in life."

"Maybe you're right," Grace shrugged. "But if you want the finer things, maybe you should work for them yourself. Regardless, you're unlikely to find what you're looking for here."

"We'll just see about that—"

"Enough, Valerie," Cole said from the side of the barn. Grace and Valerie turned to see him leaning up against his truck, his arms crossed over his chest. His cowboy hat shaded his face from view, but his tone of voice made it crystal clear he was unhappy.

"Baby, there you are," she said, her voice dripping with honey as she moved toward him.

Grace watched with interest as Cole held up his hand, stopping Valerie in her tracks. "I've told you more times than I can count that you're not welcome here," he growled. "If I see you here again, you'll leave in the back of a police car."

"You don't mean that," Valerie pouted. "We had a good thing, you and me, and we can have it again."

"It's been eight years since you left, Valerie. I have moved on with my life, and there is absolutely nothing you can say or do that will get me to change my mind. Now, please leave my property."

Grace was sure that Valerie was about to protest again, but she surprised them both by turning on her heel, an impressive feat given their size, and stomping away. Before she reached her car, she turned around one last time. "This isn't over," she yelled.

Cole and Grace watched as she flung herself into her small sports car and sped off in a cloud of dust, flinging gravel along the way. Unsure of whether or not she should approach him, Grace stayed where she was, suddenly very self-conscious of how she looked and smelled.

"I'm sorry about that," Cole said, breaking the silence.

"It's not the first time I've had to deal with an overzealous ex," Grace shrugged. She looked at the ground as embarrassment heated her cheeks. How long had he been standing there? Valerie's comments about rolling around in poop and dressing like a hobo flashed through her head. The worst part was that they were true. Well, minus the rolling around in horse poop. Cole would have had to have been blind not to notice the difference between her and Valerie.

"Hey," he said, lifting her chin with his finger until their eyes met. "Whatever you're thinking, you need to stop. It's not true."

"Are you a mind reader now?" she retorted, her voice a mixture of sassiness and sheepishness.

Cole frowned. "Your emotions are written all over your face. At some point, you'll have to learn to trust me, Grace. We can't go on like this forever."

"I don't know what you mean," she stammered.

"You keep comparing yourself to other women and somehow always find yourself lacking. I'm with you because I want to be. Because I think you're beautiful and sweet, smart, capable, and most importantly, because I love you. I don't want Valerie or any other woman; I want you. Please accept that already."

Grace felt thoroughly chastised and tried to look away, but he wouldn't let her. "I'm sorry," she muttered.

He let go of her face and pulled her close to him. "I don't want you to be sorry," he sighed. "I want you to trust me. To trust my feelings for you."

"I do trust you, Cole," she whispered into his chest. "It's just that next to Valerie, I feel like a mule standing next to a thoroughbred."

She heard him chuckle as his arms wrapped tighter around her waist. "The only thing you have in common with a mule is your stubbornness."

"Hey!" she said as she playfully swatted his chest. "I am not stub—" His lips were on hers before she could finish her sentence, and by the time they came up for air, she had entirely forgotten what she had planned to say.

"I'm afraid I have to go, baby girl," Cole said, disappointment clear on his face. "But I'll be by later this evening and we can finally spend some time together."

"That would be great!" Grace replied enthusiastically. "Do you have time for that, though? Now that you've taken over Ray's farm, you've barely had time to breathe, much less come by to see me."

"I've got a guy coming by in a little bit to interview for a farmhand position. As long as he's at least halfway competent, I'm going to hire him. The extra help should hopefully free up some time, and I can think of only one way I wish to spend it."

He kissed her again, long and slow, causing her to shiver a little despite the heat. "In that case," she said when they broke apart, "I'll have your favorite dinner ready when you arrive."

"Sounds good, but I'm far more interested in dessert..." he winked at her, then gave her one final kiss. "I'll see you later, darlin'."

Not trusting herself to respond, she smiled and gave him a little wave before driving down the gravel drive. As she went, she thought about her earlier confrontation with Valerie, and if she was honest, she didn't blame the woman for wanting Cole back. Instead, she blamed her for ever letting him go in the first place. A mistake that Grace herself would never make.

***

When Grace got home, she found Molly pacing in the dining room, her surprise quickly turning to concern when she saw how agitated her friend was. "What's wrong?" Grace asked. "Is it Granny? Gladys? The baby?" Her eyes were immediately drawn to Molly's small but pronounced baby bump.

Molly stopped in her tracks and turned to face Grace, despair written clearly on her face. "Oh, Grace, I'm so sorry," she said, her words coming out in a rush. Then, when she saw the look on Grace's face, she put her hands up. "Oh no, I'm doing it again. Everyone is fine," she quickly assured her friend.

It took a minute for Grace's heartbeat to return to normal, her confusion over Molly's behavior wreaking havoc on her nerves. "Can we sit down, please?" she asked, certain the stress of whatever was going on could not be good for the baby.

While Molly sat down, Grace hurried to put a kettle of water on the stove to heat, then joined her at the table. "Let's start at the beginning. What has made you so upset?"

Molly took a deep breath and let it out slowly. "I put the wrong dates on the Mother's Day Experience package," she said as she shook her head. "I don't know what happened, pregnancy brain, I guess."

Grace had known Molly for almost six months and had never known her to be anything less than meticulous with details. "What dates did you put down?" she asked nervously.

"I thought Mother's Day was on the seventh instead of the fourteenth. So, the guests are scheduled to arrive on the fifth instead of the twelfth."

"But that's tomorrow," Grace gasped. The sound of the kettle whistling interrupted the start of her panic attack, and she quickly got up to grab it. Back at the table, with two teacups in hand, she tried again to make sense of the latest predicament. "Okay, so we'll celebrate Mother's Day a week early. I guess that's not the end of the world."

"That's not all," Molly winced. "I sort of forgot to put an end date. So the guests expect to be here from Friday the fifth until Monday the fifteenth."

"Please tell me this is a joke." When Molly hung her head, Grace knew she was serious. "That means we'll have to feed and entertain ten people for ten days. Shall I assume they only paid for three of those ten since the dates got messed up?"

"Financially, I think we'll be okay. I raised the prices since we're starting to get a pretty good following, which will help, and I'll do my best to negotiate discounts with some of the bigger businesses. Of course, that doesn't make up for the extra cooking and cleaning you'll have to do, but I swear I'll help as much as possible. I really am sorry," she blew out her breath, causing her bangs to fly up.

It was difficult, but Grace managed to suppress the urge to scream. People made mistakes; she had certainly made her fair share, and getting upset would solve nothing. "It's okay. Right now, we need to focus on getting ready for the guests," she looked at her watch. "It's almost time for breakfast; once that's done, I need to clean the bedrooms and the bathrooms. Luckily, I did a deep clean after the Easter guests left, so I only need to make the beds, dust, and vacuum. After that, I'll need to clean the downstairs areas."

"What can I do to help?"

"Honestly? The biggest problem we're going to have is entertainment. We already have plans for next weekend, so we need something for them to do in the meantime. The city has a lot more options than we do, so if you can try to find some activities, that would be really helpful."

"I can help clean, too. This is my mistake, Grace. You shouldn't have to pay for it."

"That's very kind of you, but I'm not doing anything I wouldn't have done anyway. The only difference is I'm doing it a week early. The cleaning I can handle; it's the rest that's giving me heart palpitations."

Molly looked at her hesitantly. "If you're sure..." she trailed off.

"Trust me, I'm sure. You definitely have the more difficult job." Grace got up and took their empty teacups to the sink. "I'm going to start breakfast," she called over her shoulder. "The rest of the gang should be here soon. Maybe they'll have some suggestions of things the guests can do."

"Thanks for being so understanding," Molly said with a small smile. "I was certain you were going to want to kill me."

"I'll admit I was tempted," Grace returned her smile. "But it's okay. Nothing to do now but make it work."

"You really are the best." Molly got out her laptop and got to work, presumably on finding things for the guests to do.

Days till Mother's Day

-Nine

O nce Grace finished the morning chores, she headed straight to the local grocery store to stock up on food for her way-too-soon-to-be-arriving guests. It would have been nice to have time to plan a menu and then shop accordingly, but at this point, she would have to take what she could get. Once everyone arrived and settled, she could see about setting aside some time for menu planning and a big shopping trip up in the city.

Back home, she quickly put up the groceries and assembled a couple of appetizer trays for when her guests arrived. She had no idea when that would be, but wanted to be prepared as much as possible at such short notice. When the door rang around noon, she wiped her hands on her pants, did her best to tamp down her nerves, and plastered as big a smile as she could muster on her face.

Nothing could have prepared her for what she saw when she opened the door. Standing on the other side was none other than Rebekah Rutherford, the woman her ex-boyfriend dumped her for, and Valerie, Cole's ex-wife. In addition to those two were two other women, both older and presumably their mothers.

"What are you doing here?" Grace asked. Her shock at seeing her nemeses on her porch caused her to momentarily forget her manners.

The older woman beside Rebekah looked at Grace over the rim of her designer sunglasses. "Is this not the Bed and Breakfast with the Mother's Day Experience?" she asked, disdain dripping from her voice.

"Um, yes, it is," Grace stammered nervously. "But I would have noticed a reservation made by someone with the last name Rutherford. Or the last name Thornton," Grace said to Valerie.

"My name is Amelia Parrish," she said. "I am Hunter's mother."

Grace was still confused. She would have definitely recognized that name and immediately declined the reservation. Even Molly, with her 'pregnancy brain,' would have noticed that. "I don't have a reservation for someone with that name."

"Of course you don't. I used my maiden name," she sniffed, as if that should have been obvious.

"Well, I'm very sorry, but this is not going to work. There is a very nice hotel about thirty minutes from here that I'm sure you'll all love. If you give me a minute, I'll get the address for you." She started to close the door, but the woman with Valerie put her foot in the way before she could.

"See here, Missy. We have already paid for our reservations, so you have no choice but to let us in and honor them."

"I am more than happy to refund your money, ma'am. In fact, I'll have it done before you reach the hotel."

"This is unacceptable," Amelia exclaimed. "Young lady, if you do not stop with this foolishness, I will call my lawyer and have him immediately file a lawsuit against you for discrimination and damages. The cost of our plane tickets from New York alone will likely bankrupt you."

"New York? I thought you were supposed to be in Scotland?" asked Grace. Surely this woman did not come all the way from Scotland just to harass her.

"I don't know what you're talking about. Why on earth would I be in Scotland?"

"Hunter told me you and your husband had gone to stay with your daughter and your new grandchild." Was this really Hunter's mom, or was Rebekah playing a trick on her?

"Hunter is an only child. You must be thinking of one of your other paramours. I've heard you have several."

If looks could kill, Grace was pretty sure she would be dead. Hunter's mom—if it really is his mom—was clearly holding a grudge. About what, Grace had no idea, but she had a feeling this was going to be the worst week of her life. And she hadn't even gotten to Valerie yet.

"I'm dead, aren't I? And this is Hell. The preachers got it all wrong. Hell is not fire and brimstone; it's being forced to spend eternity catering to your enemies in your own home."

Rebekah rolled her eyes. "Stop being so dramatic and show us to our rooms." She pushed Grace out of the way and stomped up the stairs, the rest of the women following close behind.

Of course, they all left their luggage on the porch, likely expecting Grace to lug it up to their rooms for them. With a sigh, she grabbed Amelia's and trudged up the stairs after them. To the surprise of no one—especially Grace—she found the women arguing over who should get the 'nicer' room, even though four of the five rooms were of equal size and 'niceness,' the only difference being color and décor.

In the end, Amelia and Rebekah 'won' the room they were fighting for. Valerie and the woman she was with were no match for the New York socialites who had spent their entire lives getting their way. Grace might have felt sorry for them if it had been anyone else other than Valerie.

That settled, Grace followed Valerie and the mystery woman into their chosen room. "I suppose this is what you meant when you said it wasn't over?" Grace asked Valerie.

Valerie turned to face her and gave her what could only be described as a cat-that-ate-the-canary grin. "I told you I always get what I want."

Grace made a show of looking around. "Except for when you don't...."

Valerie sneered and rolled her eyes. "Anyway, let me introduce you to Anita Reed, aka Cole's mom."

Anita stepped forward and bowed dramatically. It would have been humorous if it wasn't so shocking. "You're Cole's mom?" Grace asked incredulously. "And you're here with Valerie?"

"Of course I am," Anita replied, as if it should have been obvious. "Valerie is my daughter-in-law."

"Was your daughter-in-law," Grace corrected. "Eight years ago. Before she cheated on your son and left him for 'greener pastures.'"

Anita shrugged. "Valerie has assured me she's changed, and I believe her."

Grace shook her head. In the time she'd known Cole, he had never once mentioned his mother—the reason why was quickly becoming apparent. "I cannot for the life of me figure out your plan or why you think staying at the B&B will somehow change Cole's mind about you, but whatever. If you'll excuse me, I need to prepare for the other guests."

On her way out the door, they called her back. "We would like two bottles of Perrier, chilled, along with a charcuterie board delivered to our room, pronto," Valerie snapped her fingers for emphasis.

"We have an assortment of drinks and snacks laid out for you in the dining room downstairs. Please feel free to help yourselves."

"What part of delivered do you not understand?" asked Valerie.

"What part of this is a small-town bed-and-breakfast, not the Waldorf, do you not understand? Nowhere in our package details does it say we offer room service. So if you planned to spend the next week ordering me around like a servant, you're going to be highly disappointed." Grace shut the door behind her, but not before she glimpsed Anita standing off to the side with her phone pointed toward her. Was that their game? To record their interactions with her and use the footage to make her look bad? It wasn't a bad plan, especially if they edited it to make her look like a bully or jerk—which she had no doubt they would.

The doorbell rang, signaling the arrival of more guests. Just what she needed—an audience to her torment. If she were smart, she would record this herself and post it to YouTube. She had no doubt this nightmare would make for an entertaining reality show. If only it were as fake as the 'real' reality shows out there.

Grace usually did her best to try to guess her guests' names when they arrived, a trick she had learned from a couple of hospitality classes to make people feel more welcome and at home, but since Anita and Amelia had used fake names, she was no longer confident in her guesses. Luckily, when she opened the door this time, she didn't recognize the people on the other side.

"Welcome to Winterwood," Grace said as she extended her hand to the dark-haired woman on the porch. "I'm Grace, and I will be your hostess for the week."

The woman smiled as she shook Grace's hand. "Thank you. I'm Kate, and this is my daughter Izzie," she said, gesturing to a young woman who looked around sixteen.

Due to Mother's Day falling within the school year, Grace and Molly had assumed that all the mother-daughter duos would be adults. A teenager could present a problem with some of the activities they had scheduled—especially the trip to the winery. Oh well, that would have to be a problem for another day. "Please come in," Grace said as she stepped back out of the way. "If you follow me, I'll show you to your room."

"Oh my," Kate gasped when she stepped inside. "Your house is gorgeous. I love the details on the crown molding!"

Grace turned back to smile at the woman just in time to catch Izzie rolling her eyes. "Thank you," she replied warmly. "My great-grandfather built this house. Granny Josephine will be available at dinner if you have any questions."

"That sounds wonderful. I'm sure I'll have at least a dozen by the time dinner rolls around!"

"And she will love answering every one of them." As they walked upstairs, Piper dashed up between them, having once again escaped from Granny's room.

"Ooh, a kitten!" Izzie exclaimed. "Can I play with her?"

This time, Grace caught Kate rolling her eyes. "Of course, you can. If your mom doesn't want her in your room, you can always take her downstairs to the living room. There are lots of toys for her to play with, in addition to our dog, Ruby."

Izzie squealed in delight as she carefully scooped up the kitten. "You're just the cutest thing in the world, aren't you," she baby-talked to the kitten.

Grace and Kate continued upstairs as Izzie disappeared downstairs. "Kids these days," Kate sighed. "Bring her all the way out here for some quality mother-daughter time, and what does she do? Disappear at the first sight of an animal."

It was not unusual for Grace to meddle in the affairs of her guests, but she usually had more time to get to know them before she stuck her nose in their business. "We have tons of activities planned for you guys over the next week. So I'm sure you'll get lots of quality bonding time before you leave."

"I hope so. I only have one more year until Izzie graduates. Then it's off to college, and who knows when I'll see her again. I know it isn't possible to make up for seventeen years of what I'm sure she sees as neglect in one week, but I will certainly try."

Kate had struck a nerve, and Grace had to try extra hard not to show it. She would have given anything for the chance to spend time with her mother. Watching these two squander a relationship Grace herself had never been allowed to have would be worse than anything Rebekah and Valerie could dream up combined. She gulped down her feelings and smiled at the woman. "All you can do is try. We'll certainly do our best to help in any way we can."

Too emotional to continue, she left Kate in her room and headed back downstairs just as the doorbell rang for the third time. The other two mother-daughter duos had arrived. "Welcome to Winterwood!" Grace said to the four women on her porch.

The women, who had been chatting when Grace opened the door, turned their attention to her. "Nice to meet you," a woman who looked to be in her sixties replied. "I'm Julie, and this is my daughter Journee," she said, pointing to the woman beside her. The two were in matching t-shirts, making their connection hard to miss.

Journee smiled and held out her hand. "Mom was a big fan of the band," she said with a laugh.

"I will try to keep my Journey comments to a minimum," Grace said, immediately liking the woman who, at first glance, appeared to be in her forties.

"I'm Stella, and this is Violet," the other woman said. She was reserved but polite, her young daughter smiling shyly from behind her.

Violet looked to be in her late teens or early twenties, and Grace hoped she would get along well with Izzie. The group was a mixed bag, age- and personality-wise, but that had worked well in the past, and she hoped this time would be no different. Well, at least for the three normal duos. With Valerie and Rebekah in the mix, anything could and probably would happen.

She led them inside and up the stairs to their rooms, grateful to hear their exclamations of excitement when they saw where they would be staying for the next week. Once everyone was settled, she gave a tour of the house, ending in the dining room where the drinks and snacks had been set up. Despite their earlier demands for refreshments, Valerie and Anita had opted out of the tour. To Grace's surprise, Amelia and Rebekah had joined the group and appeared to be having a good time conversing with some of the other women. Maybe things wouldn't be so bad after all.

Days till Mother's Day

-Eight-

As soon as the alarm went off, Grace hurried downstairs to put the coffee on and set out fruit and muffins. She didn't anticipate any of her guests getting up before she got back, but she wanted to be prepared, just in case. When she entered the kitchen, she was surprised to see Rebekah sitting at the dining room table with a cup of tea. "Rough night?" she asked her.

Rebekah glanced up at her with sleep-deprived eyes. "You have no idea."

"Something wrong with your room?" Grace asked cautiously. The last thing she wanted to do was give Rebekah an opening to start complaining—especially since that's all she did the last time she stayed there.

"If you ever repeat this, I swear I will deny it and leave you to face Amelia's wrath alone, but she snores. Loudly. I tried as hard as I could to ignore it, but it sounded like a freight train barreling down the tracks toward me. So I finally gave up and came down here for some much-needed peace and quiet."

Grace chuckled at the image. "I'm sorry to hear that. Maybe we can get some noise-canceling headphones or some earplugs or something."

Rebekah eyed her suspiciously. "I expected you to revel in my misery. What gives?"

"Despite beliefs to the contrary, I do not enjoy the misery of others," Grace shrugged. "I would, however, like to know why you're here. I haven't seen or heard from Hunter since Valentine's Day. So what is it the two of you hope to accomplish by coming here?"

"Honestly? I have no idea. Amelia and Richard—Hunter's father," Rebekah explained, "are looking for someone to blame for Hunter's 'rebellion.' Unfortunately, that person is you."

"Me?" Grace asked, her hand to her heart. "Why are they blaming me? And what does that even mean? What are they going to do to me?"

"I'm not sure what the plan is; I'm just as innocent as you are."

Grace raised her brow. "For some reason, I find that hard to believe." She looked at her watch and cringed. "I need to get over to the ranch. I'll happily listen to your tale of woe if you'd like to come along. Or you can stay here and hide from Amelia. The choice is yours."

Rebekah looked down at her designer sweatpants and T-shirt. "I can't go out in public like this. What will people think?"

"If by people you mean the horses, I doubt they're going to care," she replied dryly. It was tempting to point out her own outfit, but after the way Valerie had described her the other day, she felt it prudent not to highlight her lack of fashion skills.

"Fine, let's go. Anything is better than listening to that woman snore."

Five minutes later, they pulled up to Cole's ranch and parked in front of the house. Grace watched from the corner of her eye as Rebekah looked around. She expected to hear a lot of snide remarks and sarcastic comments and was pleasantly surprised when Rebekah smiled instead.

"It looks just like the pictures I've seen with the cute farmhouse and red barn," she exclaimed. "I can see why you like coming here," she said wistfully.

"I'm very lucky," Grace said softly. She looked around the ranch with new eyes. It was amazing how easy it was to take things for granted. Finally, after a few moments of silence, she got out of the car and led the way over to the barn. "If you want, you can sit over there on a hay bale. I should be able to hear you talk while I work."

"You don't expect me to help?"

"You want to shovel horse poop?" Grace raised her brow. She laughed when Rebekah quickly shook her head. "I didn't think so." When Rebekah was settled, Grace began her inquisition. "Why don't you tell me why Hunter lied about having a sister?"

Rebekah sighed. "It was a game we used to play when we were kids. I have an older brother, but he's ten years older than me, so I was practically raised as an only child. Hunter and I would pretend we had siblings and, more importantly, 'normal' parents."

"Normal parents?" Grace asked as she piled the poop into the wagon. "What does that mean?"

"Look, I know that I was fortunate to grow up rich and that there are struggles that I have never had to face. But people like Hunter and I were raised to live exactly how our parents wanted. We were never allowed to have dreams of our own—hobbies, careers, or even to date the people we wanted to date. Our parents decided when we were young that Hunter and I would get married when we were older. They wanted to keep the wealth in the family."

"In the family? You guys aren't related, are you?"

"No, not by blood. But our families go back generations. From the time we were born, they had our lives mapped out. Hunter would take over his father's business, and I would become his socialite wife."

"So what happened?"

"My parents didn't think it was necessary for me to go to college, so they allowed me to travel instead. They thought it would help me become more 'worldly' and give me experience and knowledge for my future fundraising days. In other words, they expected me to join my mother on all her charity boards when I became Hunter's wife. Hunter, meanwhile, went to college and majored in finance, just like his dad. For a couple of years, he worked his way up the corporate ladder at his dad's company. Then, last Christmas, everything came to a head." She took a deep breath as if reliving the scene in her head.

Grace had so many questions she wanted to ask but was too afraid to interrupt. So she kept quiet and continued shoveling as she processed the information.

"Hunter and I turned twenty-five last year, and our parents decided it was time for us to get married. So they called me home and told me my days of traveling the world were over. I'm not sure what they told Hunter, but whatever it was caused him to disappear—or, as we later learned, come out here to your B&B."

"And the story about his made-up sister and niece?"

"That was the family he wished he had. An older sister who would have taken some of the pressure off him, and two parents who loved them enough to move to Scotland to be a part of their daughter and granddaughter's lives."

"It's sad he felt he needed to lie to me. I would have tried to understand."

"You think you could have understood that Hunter had a fiancée back home? That would have put a damper on your romantic feelings, don't you think?"

There was a bitterness to her words that had Grace thinking back to some of their conversations on Valentine's Day. Grace had assumed that Hunter had cheated on her with Rebekah, but the truth was Hunter had cheated on Rebekah with Grace. Suddenly, she didn't feel so self-righteous. "I'm sorry, Rebekah. I didn't know. If I did, I never would have allowed a relationship..." she trailed off, not wanting to make things worse.

"It's okay," Rebekah replied after a few minutes of silence. "I don't think either of us wanted to get married; it was just so ingrained in us from such an early age we honestly felt like we had no choice. What bothered me the most was that he had the courage to defy our parents, and I didn't. I was too afraid of getting cut off and actually having to stand on my own two feet. What would I even do? My parents financed everything I did."

"From what Molly told me, you were a successful influencer. Don't people like that make a lot of money?"

Rebekah shrugged. "Yes, but not the kind of money my parents have. And not consistently, either. It was too scary to contemplate giving that up."

"So what happened? After Hunter went back to New York, I mean."

"My parents and I ran into him on the street. It snowballed from there. They called Hunter's parents, and the next thing we knew, they started planning the wedding. Hunter and I talked about running away, but I couldn't go through with it. Then I found out he had left to return here, so I followed him."

"Before he left, Hunter told me he would travel with you around the world and help with your business. So I guess that was a lie, too?"

Nodding, Rebekah pulled up a piece of hay and began twirling it between her fingers. "He agreed to return to New York with me but never showed up. When I got back home, he was gone, and our parents were furious. He had called and told them he wasn't coming back."

"Wow, I can't imagine how hard that must have been. But what does Amelia hope to accomplish by coming here? Surely she doesn't think I'm hiding him in the cellar or something?"

"This is the last place they know to look for him," she said. She pulled at another piece of hay and stuck it in her mouth absentmindedly.

It was so tempting to take a picture of her, but Grace didn't want to mess up their temporary truce, so she kept her phone in her pocket. "I can promise you he isn't here. At least, to my knowledge, he isn't. I have no idea where to even begin to look for him. So much of what he told me about himself was a lie; I'm beginning to think I never really knew him at all."

"Hey, Grace," Cole called out. He walked into the barn and stopped when he saw Rebekah, causing the tall, blond-haired man behind him to bump into him. "Rebekah, this is certainly a surprise. Never in a million years would I have expected to see you sitting in my barn."

"Hi, Cole," she said somewhat shyly. "I'm not trying to intrude or anything; I'm just hanging out with Grace."

"Something else I thought I'd never see." He looked at Grace questioningly, but she just shrugged. "Anyway, I want to introduce you to Riley," he said, gesturing toward the blond-haired man. "I hired him to help me out around here."

Grace watched with interest as Riley and Rebekah's eyes met. She was sure she saw literal sparks fly between them and was amused to see the usually bold and bossy Rebekah turn into a shy, bashful woman.

"I thought you told me I wouldn't run into anyone," she whispered furiously to Grace.

"It's nice to meet you, Riley," Grace said, ignoring Rebekah. "I'm thrilled that Cole will finally have some help around here."

"Looks like he's already got help," Riley smiled as he gestured toward the wagon full of manure. "Not many women out there willing to get up at the crack of dawn to help their man out."

"That's what partners do, isn't that right, Grace?" Rebekah said quickly.

Grace smiled and nodded to keep from laughing at Rebekah's blatant attempt to look good in front of Riley. The last thing she wanted to do was give the woman a reason to hang around, but a little harmless flirting could be good for her. It might even make her more agreeable, if her current attitude was any indication.

"I'm afraid it's going to be another long night," Cole told Grace. "But we should have some time for a barbecue tomorrow if you want?"

"I would love nothing more, but your mom and Valerie are staying at the B&B." She watched his face as a myriad of emotions played out, none of them good.

"Sounds like we have some things to discuss later," he finally said, his teeth clenched.

"The guests are supposed to go to the city tomorrow to have lunch and see a matinee at the theater. You guys could come over then for that barbecue?"

"Fine, I'll see you then," he walked away without kissing her goodbye, something he hadn't done in a long time.

"See you guys later," Riley waved as he followed Cole.

"Looks like I'm not the only one with some family drama," Rebekah said, her eyes on Riley.

"Tomorrow is sure to be an interesting day," Grace mumbled absentmindedly.

"What's on the agenda for today?"

"Extreme mini-golf." Grace smiled when she saw Rebekah's face. "The itinerary was made before we knew who was coming. It's the kind of thing a man like Riley would love," Grace said innocently.

"How would you know?"

"Because Cole is the one who told me about it."

"Hmph, are you going?"

"Yes, I'll be the one driving the bus. If nothing else, watching Valerie ride the zip-line in her patented four-inch heels will be entertaining!"

They both giggled at the image. "I have a feeling she's going to be worse than I was on Valentine's Day."

"She's certainly giving it her best shot."

"At least it's only for a week," Rebekah said cheerfully.

"From your lips to God's ears." Grace wanted to believe her but couldn't quite bring herself to do it. Valerie had hung around much longer than either she or Cole had expected. Since it was unlikely she was doing it out of love, the only possibility was that the woman had exhausted all her other options. That made her desperate, and desperate people tended to do desperate things.

Suddenly, Grace found herself wishing for simpler times. Even things with Dot hadn't seemed this bleak, and that woman had her fearing for her safety. Oh well, not much she could do about it.

-Seven-

G race stood at the kitchen counter mixing ingredients for her famous stuffed French toast. It had been a while since she'd had time to think and process the events of the last couple of days. At some point in the middle of the night, Rebekah knocked on her door and practically begged Grace to let her bunk with her for the night. Her petty side had wanted to tell her no; after all, it wasn't that long ago Rebekah had made her life a living nightmare. However, even less time had passed since Grace had been a victim of sleepless nights, so in the end, her compassionate side won out.

When the alarm went off at five-thirty, Rebekah again surprised her by rolling out of bed and tagging along on her trip to the ranch. She claimed she would help out as a thank you, but Grace had a feeling her newfound magnanimous side had more to do with a certain blond-haired cowboy and less to do with any actual appreciation for Grace's generosity. Regardless of her motive, Grace accepted her help.

The extreme mini-golf event the previous day had been a success. As predicted, Valerie had dressed for the club but handled all the challenges like a pro. It truly had been a sight to see when she jumped off the zip-line and landed on her feet in four-inch heels. How she managed to convince the worker to let her do it, Grace would never know, but she would give props where they were due.

Amelia had come down with a conveniently timed migraine right before they were about to leave and had stayed home to 'rest.' Grace liked to imagine her crawling around down in the crawl space looking for signs that Hunter was there—cobwebs in her perfectly coiffed hair, her immaculate pantsuit covered in dirt. A part of her did feel sorry for the woman; after all, not knowing where her only child was had to be torture. But if what Rebekah had said was true, maybe it was time for Amelia to learn that consequences weren't just for people with low incomes.

Her ingredients mixed, she moved to the preheated pan on the stove and started dipping the bread in the mixture and laying it on the pan. She liked to use French bread for stuffed French toast—the thicker pieces of bread cutting some of the sweetness of the cream cheese.

Just as she was putting the finishing touches on the plates of food, the guests appeared and plopped down in the chairs around the table. "Good morning, everyone," Grace said as she placed plates of food in front of them.

"What's this?" Valerie asked, her face scrunched up as if she'd been handed a plate of dirty socks.

"Stuffed French toast with strawberries, bacon, sausage, and orange juice," Grace replied pleasantly. It was going to be one of those days; she could already tell.

"You expect me to eat this?" Valerie asked incredulously. "It's nothing but carbs." She looked Grace up and down. "As you should know by now, carbs go straight to the midsection."

"We're on vacation," Journee chimed in around a mouthful of food. "Everyone knows that vacation calories don't count."

Valerie gave her a disgusted look, but she shut up and picked up her fork and knife, cutting off the tiniest sliver of French toast possible and sticking it in her mouth. "Eww," she said. "This tastes like it's burnt. Can't you do anything right?" she asked Grace.

"Looks just like mine, and mine's perfect," Journee interjected again. "I'll take it if you don't want it."

"Fine," she said, pushing her plate across the table. "I guess I'll just starve."

Grace sighed. "Is there something else I can make you?" she asked the ridiculous woman. It was clear, at least to Grace, that Valerie would have found fault with whatever was given to her. Out of the corner of her eye, she saw Anita once again pointing her phone at Grace. Whatever their plan, it was not likely to end well.

"I'll take a western-style omelet, hash browns, and two slices of turkey bacon."

"That sounds good; I'll have the same," Anita said, pushing her plate away from her.

"You know what, I think I'll have that as well," said Amelia.

This was not the way things were supposed to go. Yes, most hotels offered several options for breakfast, but Grace had never done that. She had minimal experience as a cook and preferred to keep things simple; that way, there were fewer chances of something going wrong. Until now, it had never been a problem, and while she would have loved nothing more than to tell these people where they could shove their omelets, the rest of the guests were watching, so she put a smile on her face and grinned through her annoyance.

"Anyone else?" she asked as she looked around the table. Then, when no one spoke up, she turned around and returned to the kitchen to make their order.

Fifteen minutes later, she brought the food to the table. Valerie took one bite and then shoved the plate away. "I think I'll save my appetite for the meal we're supposed to have at the theater."

"Better make sure you eat your fill," replied Anita. "It will be the last time you get any 'real' food for at least a few days."

It took every ounce of strength Grace had not to point out how the two of them had stuffed their faces the day before. Instead, she smiled through gritted teeth as they stood up and left the room.

"I wouldn't mind having that as a snack later if you want to save it for me," Julie said, pointing to the omelet.

"Me too," said Journee. "No sense in letting good food go to waste."

Grace smiled, a genuine smile this time, as she cleared the plates. "Thank you. I would be happy to box these up for you. Let me know when you want them, and I'll reheat them for you."

The rest of the guests, now finished with their breakfast, got up and left—most of them, it appeared, heading back to their rooms, likely to get ready for the play. As she cleaned the dishes, Rebekah approached, causing her to groan inwardly.

"Was I that bad?" Rebekah asked sheepishly.

Surprised, Grace thought about it for a minute. "No, you weren't that bad. You were close, but not even you were that condescending and obnoxious."

"I'm glad to hear that...I think." She picked up a towel and dried the pans Grace had washed by hand.

"We can't change the past; all we can do is try our best going forward. I won't pretend to understand your situation, but you have choices, Rebekah."

"I wish that were true," she sighed. "Are the guys still coming over after everyone leaves?"

"As far as I know, yes. Why? Are you thinking about staying behind?"

"I'm not much of a play person..." she trailed off, her cheeks flushing.

Grace turned her head to hide her smile. "I see. Well, you're welcome to join us. Although, with the way Cole reacted to the news of his mother being here..." it was her turn to trail off, the meaning behind her words clear.

"Hopefully, it will all work out in the end."

Their eyes met for a moment before Rebekah turned to leave. "I'm going to check on Amelia and make sure she's going to the play. I'll see you later."

Before Grace could respond, she was gone.

***

Grant and Molly showed up at eleven with the bus they had rented to transport everyone to the theater in the city. Gladys and Granny had decided to stay home, citing their various ailments as an excuse to avoid the long outing. Once again, Amelia had opted out and had disappeared an hour or so earlier, taking off for parts unknown in her rental car. Her quest to find Hunter had turned into a literal Where in the World is Carmen Sandiego game.

Cole pulled up to the curb just as Grant pulled away. Grace watched from the porch as Valerie's face appeared in the window at the back of the bus. It was hard to tell from a distance, but it looked like she was screaming—likely at Grant to stop the bus. Unfortunately for her, Grant kept going, and Grace was treated to the sight of her nemesis pounding on the back of the window in frustration. It was the little things that helped her get through the day.

Better still, Cole didn't even glance in Valerie's direction, which only upset her further. Grace knew laughing was childish, but she couldn't help herself. However, the look on Cole's face caused her to sober up pretty quickly. "You don't look very happy to see me," she said nervously.

"It's not you," he said as he ran his hand over his face.

Rebekah stepped outside and joined them on the porch just as Riley approached from the walkway. "Hey, ladies," he said with a grin. "It's nice to see you both again."

As if sensing the tension, Rebekah looked from Grace to Cole, then Riley. "Hey, I was just about to go for a walk. Would you like to join me?" she asked.

"Sure. You guys don't mind, do you?" he asked Grace and Cole.

They shook their heads in unison, then waited in silence until the duo had walked far enough away to no longer be able to hear them. "I have enchiladas in the oven," Grace said, breaking the silence. "I thought you might prefer something simpler to a barbecue."

Cole looked at her for a minute and then pulled her into his arms, resting his head on top of hers. "Thank you," he said quietly.

They stayed like that for a while, neither wanting to let go. Then, finally, he stepped back and led her by the hand over to the wicker couch on the side of the porch. "I feel like I owe you an explanation," he said as he pulled her beside him. He wrapped his arm around her shoulder and pulled her close.

"I'm just sorry this upset you so much," Grace replied. "It's not fun for me either, but I can't imagine how you feel knowing your mom is in cahoots with your ex."

"That's just it," he said bitterly. "I have no idea who Valerie conned into helping her out, but she's not my mother."

Grace sat up and looked at him, a stunned expression on her face. "Are you sure? I mean, trying to pass a stranger off as your mother seems risky. All it would take is for you to come over one time and see the woman to blow whatever their plan is to bits."

"My mother passed away two years ago from cancer," he said softly.

The anguish on his face was so raw it took her breath away while simultaneously breaking her heart. "Oh, Cole." She threw her arms around his neck and hugged him tightly. "I'm so sorry. Why didn't you tell me?"

He sighed deeply. "I don't know. It never came up, and after what you went through, losing both of your parents at such a young age, I guess I just never knew how to broach the subject."

"My pain does not supersede yours," she said softly. "Besides, I've had twenty years to process my grief; you've only had two."

"It's not a contest."

"No, it isn't. And I don't want you to feel like you can't share your feelings with me. Especially ones like this." She thought about it for a minute, her compassion turning to anger. "Does Valerie know?"

"I have no idea. I would like to believe the answer is no, and that not even she could be that cruel and heartless."

"I hope you're right. Regardless, it's a pretty crummy thing to do."

"Yeah, and one my mother would never have agreed to. She never cared for Valerie. I should have listened to her."

Rebekah and Riley reappeared, walking much closer together than two people who had just met usually would. "What do you make of them?" Grace asked Cole, grateful for the distraction from the painful topic they had been discussing.

Cole shrugged. "So far, Riley seems to be a good guy. He's a hard worker and easy to get along with. He's looking to settle down, though. Spent the last ten years traveling the country on the rodeo circuit and is tired of that kind of life."

"I suspect Rebekah is looking for the same thing."

"Oh?" He raised his brow. "I thought she was some kind of travel blogger?"

"There have been some new developments I haven't had a chance to tell you about," she explained. "I suspect she's spent the last few years traveling the world searching for a home."

"I can see that," he nodded. "Guess we'll have to see how it goes."

Grace stood up when they reached the porch. "Y'all ready for lunch?" she asked the group.

"I'm starving," Riley replied enthusiastically.

Rebekah led the way inside, offering to set the table and grab everyone's drinks. Grace started to follow when Cole grabbed her hand and pulled her back against his chest. "She would have loved you, you know," he whispered in her ear.

"Your mom?" she asked, craning her neck to look up at him.

He nodded in response, then kissed her deeply, his arms circling her waist and holding her tightly.

"I have a feeling I would have loved her too," she whispered when they broke apart.

"I love you, Grace."

"I love you, too."

"Guess we better get inside. I'm interested to see this new domestic side of Rebekah's. Think it's just for show? To impress Riley, I mean?"

"Probably. Although she did help me this morning when no one else was around, so who knows? At this point, I'll take what I can get; motives be danged."

Cole grabbed her hand and led her inside, where the sound of laughter greeted them. Granny and Gladys had decided to join them for lunch and, from the sound of things, were regaling Rebekah and Riley with tales from their previous adventures with Dot and her gang of elderly misfits. The sight of everyone laughing and having a good time made Grace smile. These were the times she would treasure for the rest of her life. Everything else was just background noise.

-Six-

Back in the kitchen, Grace whipped up various breakfast food options as she daydreamed about exposing Valerie and Anita for the frauds they were. The group had stayed out later than planned the day before, leaving little time for vengeance when they finally made it back and crashed in their respective rooms. This may have been a good thing since Grace wasn't sure she wanted to air her dirty laundry in front of her unsuspecting guests.

"I sure hope the look on your face has nothing to do with me," Rebekah smirked as she sat on a stool.

"Just dreaming about ways to get back at Valerie," Grace replied.

"If you ask me, you should wait and let it all play out. Now that you know she's lying, it seems this could be more entertaining than infuriating."

"I suppose you have a point," Grace conceded. "Now that I no longer need to worry about her making me look bad in front of Cole, I guess it no longer matters what she does."

Rebekah rolled her eyes. "You never had to worry about her making you look bad. That man is head over heels in love with you. You're as crazy as she is if you thought she had a chance of coming between the two of you."

"You mean that?" Grace asked uncertainly.

"Do I look like the kind of woman that gives fake platitudes?"

She had a point. Despite her recent changes for the better, Rebekah was still a bit of a diva at heart. "No, I suppose you're not...." Grace trailed off.

"Exactly. Besides, I'd give my right arm to have a guy look at me the way Cole looks at you. If it were me, I'd spend less time worrying about people like Valerie and more time on getting that man to put a ring on it." She pointed to her wedding ring finger for emphasis.

"Hey guys," Journee called out when she entered the kitchen. She sat down on a stool next to Rebekah. "What is going on with that Valerie chick?"

Grace handed her a cup of coffee. "What do you mean?"

"She went nuts on the bus yesterday when we left your house. She was hootin' and hollerin' about her baby being left behind. The thing is, I haven't seen nor heard a baby since I got here. I was wondering if we need to get her some help or something."

It was difficult, but she managed to control her urge to burst out laughing—that is, until she made the mistake of looking at Rebekah. When she finally got herself under control, the look on Journee's face sent her back over the edge. "I'm so sorry," she said, wiping the tears from her eyes. "While I do think she needs some help, Valerie was referring to my boyfriend, not an actual baby."

"Oh," she looked relieved. "I can see why you thought that was funny." She went silent for a minute. "Wait, why is she calling your boyfriend her baby?"

"Cole, my boyfriend, is her ex-husband," Grace explained. "She's decided she wants him back even though eight years have passed, and he's moved on."

"Hmm, well, if you're referring to that hunk of a man in the cowboy hat and black truck, I can't say I blame her. I'm not sure carrying on like that and screaming like a banshee is the best way to go about things, though."

Grace raised her brow. "No, I would say not. I, however, would like to believe it wouldn't matter how she acted." She busied herself taking muffins out of the oven and setting them on racks to cool.

"I'm sorry; I didn't mean it like that," Journee apologized. "My brain needs at least two cups of coffee before it's fully functioning in the morning."

The poor woman looked so embarrassed Grace immediately took pity on her. "It's alright. You're supposed to be on vacation, yet here you are with front-row seats to a drama you never signed up to see. I'm the one who should be apologizing."

"Hey, now that I know I'm free to sit back and enjoy the show without worrying about the woman's mental state, it's all good."

The rest of the guests filed in, effectively ending the conversation. Having missed her chance with Cole the day before, Valerie was on the warpath. "Coffee, now," she snapped the fingers on one hand while she held out the other.

Grace rolled her eyes but dutifully poured a cup and put it in the woman's hand. Valerie shrieked and dropped the cup, sending coffee and shards of ceramic all over the counter and the food sitting on it. "What the heck!" exclaimed Grace. She quickly grabbed a rag to wipe off the mess, but it was too late; the food was ruined.

"She tried to kill me," Valerie yelled, pointing at Grace. "You're all my witnesses."

"What are you talking about?" Rebekah asked incredulously. "The only thing I witnessed is you dropping that cup and spilling coffee everywhere." She tried to mop the coffee off her blouse with a damp rag before the stain set in.

"The coffee was too hot," Valerie screamed. "She burned my hand."

"Let me see," Journee grabbed her hand. "It doesn't look burned to me."

Valerie snatched her hand back. "Since when are you a doctor?" she snapped.

"I may not be a doctor, but I am a nurse. Have been for the last two decades," Journee shrugged.

Everyone was now standing around, watching in wide-eyed silence as the scene unfolded around them. If Grace didn't get things under control fast, the whole train would derail right before her eyes. "Um," she said, clearing her throat. "How about we all pile onto the bus and drive to Addie's for breakfast?" Her voice held a hint of desperation. She hoped they were all too stunned to notice.

"I'll drive," Grant called out from the doorway.

Grace shot him a look of gratitude and watched in relief as the guests followed him out to the bus. Suddenly, Valerie's antics didn't seem so entertaining.

"Are you okay?" asked Molly.

"Yeah," Grace assured her. "Go ahead and go with them. I'm going to stay here and clean up."

"If you're sure," Molly looked uncertain.

"I'm sure, I promise. Can you bring back some food for Granny and Gladys, please? Now that all this food has been ruined, I need to run to the store again."

"Of course, I'll take my car so I can come back sooner."

"Thanks, Molly." Grace pulled out the trash can and dumped muffins and pastries into the bin.

"What can I do to help?" asked Rebekah.

Grace looked up to see she was still standing by the sink. "You should have gone with the rest of them. As I told Molly, I don't have enough ingredients to make more food until I go to the store."

"I already ate, remember? You handed me muffins straight out of the oven."

"Oh yeah, I guess I did. Could you check the floor on the other side of the counter? I'm concerned that some of the shards from the coffee cup may have ended up down there."

"Sure. What do you think that was all about?"

"I don't know," Grace shook her head. "But Anita was filming, so...."

"You think this is about more than just trying to make you look bad in front of Cole?"

"If I had to guess, I think she might be planning some sort of blackmail scheme."

Rebekah tilted her head as she thought about that. "Like, she'll threaten to post that video she's making if Cole doesn't agree to leave you for her?"

"Something like that, yeah." She grabbed a broom from the storage area and began sweeping the floor, making sure to get underneath the cabinets.

"That sounds crazy. Surely even Valerie wouldn't be crazy enough to assume that would work."

"Who knows what she thinks," Grace sighed. "Nothing else she's tried has worked, so she's probably getting desperate. I mean, she did hire an imposter to pretend to be Cole's mother. At this point, I don't think there's a level she won't stoop to."

"What's on the agenda for today?"

"Beverly agreed to do another ceramics class." Grace grimaced at the thought. "You think I should cancel?"

Rebekah looked at the mess they had almost managed to clean up. "It's risky, but probably too late to switch to something else. Hopefully, she'll behave herself since she'll be at someone else's place of business."

"Hopefully," Grace echoed, but neither one of them looked convinced.

***

To minimize the potential risk of Valerie causing a scene at Beverly's, Grace decided to stay home and let the guests go without her. Once again, Amelia disappeared after breakfast, so Grace was startled to discover her in Grace's bedroom when she went upstairs to rest. "What are you doing?" she gasped when she saw the woman rifling through her dresser drawers.

Amelia stood up so fast she swayed a little before grabbing the top of the dresser to steady herself. "I thought you were gone," she responded.

"That's all you have to say? I just caught you snooping through my things. Aren't you even a little bit embarrassed?"

"I'm looking for answers. If you had given them to me, I wouldn't have been forced to such extremes," she responded indignantly.

"I don't recall you asking any questions," Grace shot back. The woman had just been caught red-handed going through her stuff. The least she could do was apologize, but sorry did not exist in Amelia's world.

"You know why I'm here," she huffed.

"I've said this a thousand times, but for your benefit, I'm going to say it a thousand and one: Hunter is not here."

"I don't care where he isn't; I want to know where he is," Amelia crossed the room and pointed her finger in Grace's face. "And you're going to tell me," she shouted.

Grace slapped her hand away. "Your son is a grown man, not a run-away teenager. I feel for what you're going through, but can you really blame him for ghosting you? He's entitled to live his life how he sees fit, and if you can't or won't accept that, desperate times call for desperate measures."

"He wasn't like this until he met you," she spat.

"He never would have met me if he wasn't already looking for a way to escape. Blame me all you want, Amelia, but things will never change until you do."

"What do you know? You don't even have a child." Then, having lost some of her steam, she sat down on the edge of the bed and clasped her hands.

"I may not have a child, but if I did, the most important thing to me would be that they were happy. I'm sure you and your husband meant well, but Hunter wasn't happy with the life you planned for him," she said gently.

Amelia looked up at her with a wounded look in her eyes. "Richard threatened to disown him if he didn't come home and do what he was told. If I can't find Hunter and convince him to do as his father requests, I will have to choose between my husband and my son."

Tears streamed down her cheeks as her shoulders hunched. Grace had never seen another person so distraught in her entire life. Unsure of what to do, she handed her a tissue box and sat beside her. "You can always get another husband," Grace said sheepishly.

A few moments passed before Grace noticed that Amelia's shoulders had begun to shake. Concerned she had caused the woman to have a breakdown, Grace turned to comfort her only to discover she was laughing instead of crying. "Are you okay?" she asked.

Amelia waved her hand. "I can't remember the last time I had a good laugh. You kids," she sighed. "Proof that youth is wasted on the young."

"What do you mean?" Just when she thought she had made progress, Amelia insulted her again.

"That wasn't an insult," Amelia said as if reading her mind. "I just meant that it would be nice if wisdom and youth went hand in hand. Unfortunately, by the time we know better, we're usually too old to do something about it."

"I'd hardly consider you too old for anything," Grace replied. "You're a force to be reckoned with—likely will be until the day you meet your maker."

"Thank you," she said, patting her on the cheek. "I don't deserve your kindness, but it is appreciated. I'm sorry for going through your things. And for tricking you by not giving my real name when I signed up for your Mother's Day Experience."

Stunned by Amelia's sudden change of heart, Grace grabbed her hand and squeezed it. "I honestly don't know where Hunter is, but if there's anything I can do to help, please let me know."

"I think it's time I do what's best for my son and let him be. Hopefully, he'll feel strong and safe enough to contact me again someday. By that point, hopefully, I'll be strong enough too."

Amelia gave Grace's hand one last squeeze and stood up. "If you don't mind, I'm going to go lie down."

"Of course; let me know if you need anything."

She gave a curt nod and left the room, leaving Grace alone to sort through her feelings. Someday Grace hoped to hear that Amelia and Hunter had reunited and forged a new relationship. One built on mutual respect and trust. A relationship just like the one he told her about when they first met last Christmas.

-Five-

After her conversation with Amelia the day before, and with the group safely at Beverly's for the afternoon, Grace had made the trek up to the city to shop at the warehouse club. With her freezer and pantry now fully stocked, she was prepared for whatever stunt Valerie planned to pull next. Well, at least the ones regarding food.

Since the last couple of days had been high-carb, high-calorie pastry days, she decided to make today's breakfast a healthy one. She loaded a platter with fresh fruit, yogurt, and granola and set it in the middle of the table. Next, she made turkey bacon, sausage, some egg white omelets, and potatoes cooked in olive oil and sprinkled with rosemary and parmesan. Hopefully, even the pickiest of eaters could find something they liked.

As she finished setting out the food, the guests strolled into the dining room, a few talking excitedly about the upcoming trip to the winery they were going on that afternoon. "Good morning, everyone," Grace exclaimed.

"Good morning," Journee sing-songed. "It's a beautiful day today. I can't wait to head over to the winery."

"I'm glad you're excited. The owners have a special surprise planned for you that I think all of you will love!"

"Even me?" asked Izzie. She made a face that clearly indicated she was not excited and would have preferred to do almost anything other than go to the winery.

"Even you," Grace responded. "I know wineries are not typically kid-friendly, but this one is slightly different."

"In what way are they different?" asked Kate.

"They offer a line of quality sparkling grape and apple juices in addition to their wines. So there will be plenty of products to sample for those who can't or choose not to sample the wines."

"Don't worry, girlfriend," Violet said as she bumped Izzie's shoulder with her own. "I'm not old enough to drink either, so we gals will have to stick together."

Grace inwardly sighed in relief when Izzie brightened at Violet's show of camaraderie. One of her favorite parts of running the B&B was when her guests got along and had fun together. It's what made the experiences so memorable, at least to her.

"I, for one, could use a drink or ten," came a muffled response from the end of the table.

All eyes now on her, Valerie, sitting with her forehead resting on her folded arms, raised her head to glare at everyone. "This place has got to have some of the most uncomfortable beds I've ever slept on. I will never understand how you guys can be so cheerful after another night without sleep."

"Excuse me," Amelia cleared her throat. She was standing in the doorway, suitcase in hand. "Now that

I have your attention, I need to say something. I have decided to return to New York. My decision has nothing to do with Grace or my accommodations and everything to do with my need to attend to business back home. I have enjoyed my stay here and wish you all the best. Rebekah, it's time to go home."

Rebekah pushed back her chair and stood up, a look of defiance on her face. "I'm staying."

The room was so silent you could hear a pin drop as everyone waited with bated breath for the showdown to begin. Amelia stared at Rebekah for a full minute, the expressions on her face changing so rapidly they were impossible to identify. Then, finally, she nodded, turned on her heel, and left—a giant whoosh emanating from the crowd as they all released the breath they had been holding.

Grace and Rebekah exchanged a look before they rushed after her. "Let me take those bags for you," Grace said as she grabbed a bag from Amelia's hand. The three of them moved outside to where her rental car was parked and helped her load her bags into the trunk. "You don't have to leave," Grace said softly.

"I appreciate that," Amelia replied. "But I need to go home. I left a message for Hunter last night after Grace and I talked, and he called me back this morning."

"He did?" Grace and Rebekah said in unison.

Amelia nodded, a small smile briefly appearing on her usually stoic face. "He did. We agreed that things aren't working as they are and that he needs to figure out who he is away from the family and all our expectations. So I'm going to go home and get some of my affairs in order and then meet him in a couple of weeks in Scotland."

"Scotland? That's where he told me you were last Christmas," Grace said.

"I'm not sure where his obsession with Scotland came from, but it seems important to him. Who knows, maybe I'll like it too." She turned to Rebekah. "I would apologize for dragging you down here with me, but I think this is exactly where you need to be right now. The life that I, and your mother, have spent the last too many decades living is not for you. You're more than just a trophy wife, Rebekah. Don't let fear keep you from living your dreams."

They took turns hugging her goodbye, then stood by the curb watching as she drove away. "Do you think she's going to be okay?" Grace asked Rebekah.

"Yeah, I do. Amelia has her own money, so unlike me, she's not dependent on anyone to take care of her. I imagine Richard will have a new woman on his arm by the end of the week, and that will be that."

"That's a pretty sad picture you just painted," Grace pointed out.

Rebekah shrugged. "That's why Hunter and I rebelled. We didn't want that life. The question is, what am I going to do now? As soon as Amelia shows up back in New York without me, my life as I know it will officially be over."

"I don't think things are as bleak as you think. Regardless, we'll figure it out."

"We?" she asked, her brow raised.

"Yes, we. Unless you don't want my help?"

"I would love your help. I didn't think you'd want to give it after everything I've done to you."

"As I said before, it's all in the past."

They walked back inside and found the dining room had erupted into chaos. Food covered practically every surface, including the guests' hair and clothing. Some guests hid behind the counter, while others took refuge under the table. Julie, Journee, Valerie, and Anita were center stage, each with a handful of food poised mid-air.

A shrill whistle split the air, causing everyone to stop in their tracks. "What in the absolute heck is going on in here?" asked Rebekah.

Valerie and Anita had the gall to look defiant while Julie and Journee hung their heads. "We're sorry," Julie said. "We just couldn't stand another minute of that woman's nonsense."

"Nonsense," Valerie huffed. "Just because you rednecks have no standards doesn't mean we can't."

"If you find your accommodations so lacking, you're free to leave at any time," Grace deadpanned.

"Not without a full refund," Anita shot back.

"I will gladly give you a refund for the days you haven't used, minus the cost of the damages you've caused. But if you think you're going to get out of paying for those, you are sorely mistaken. A bill will be presented at the time of checkout."

"Whatever," Valerie waved her hand dismissively.

"I think everyone should return to their rooms to get cleaned up," Rebekah said. "We'll be leaving in a couple of hours."

Grace pulled out the cleaning supplies while the guests filed out. So much for the warm and fuzzy feelings they'd given her earlier. Right now, she wanted nothing more than for them all to leave.

"I'll help," Rebekah said as she grabbed the broom out of Grace's hand.

"I appreciate the offer, but you don't have to do that," Grace replied. "This mess is going to take forever to clean up."

"All the more reason for me to help."

The cleaning went relatively fast with both of them working, a fact Grace was grateful for. "I wasn't planning to drink today, but I have a feeling I'm going to need at least one glass of wine before the day is out," she told Rebekah.

"I'm with you. Although I think the whole bottle might be in order."

Grace raised an imaginary glass. "I'll drink to that!"

***

The drive to the winery was uneventful, the guests in a somewhat subdued mood as they quietly talked among themselves. While she was grateful for the break from Valerie's incessant whining, she was concerned about the overall happiness of her guests. This was supposed to be a vacation, yet it felt like a bus full of students scared of getting detention. And she was the ultra-strict teacher they feared giving it to them.

When she pulled up to the barn, Wyatt and Kenzie, the super-sweet couple who owned the winery, greeted them at the entrance. "Welcome to Vines to Wines, everyone," the couple called out cheerfully.

The group crowded around Wyatt and Kenzie as they gave a short speech about the winery and how it came to be. Once that was out of the way, they motioned for the group to follow them. "We have an awesome surprise for you guys today," Kenzie said as she led the group down a trail past the barn and out into the vineyard.

As they walked, Wyatt pointed out the different species of grapes and the types of wine or juice they were turned into. Finally, after a solid five minutes, they reached a clearing with a gorgeous view of the mini-lake. The group gasped as they took in the scene—the flowers on the nearby plants just starting to bloom, the trees with their green leaves, and the white tent with the candle-topped tables and chairs.

"It's beautiful," Kate gushed.

"Thanks," Kenzie said with a grin. "In addition to the winery, we're also a wedding venue, this being one of our most popular spots for couples to get married."

"I can see why," she said. "Next time I get married, I'm going to come here."

"We would love that!" Kenzie exclaimed. "Why don't you guys take a seat, and we'll get the wine tasting started."

In traditional Valerie fashion, instead of taking a seat as requested, she wandered off down the pier and stood at the end of it with her phone in the air, presumably to take a selfie. Since, for once, her actions seemed harmless,

Grace was prepared to let it go and took a seat with the rest of the guests. Journee, on the other hand, appeared to be holding a grudge from the morning's food fight. So, instead of taking a seat, she too walked out to the end of the pier and made a show of taking a selfie, only she 'accidentally' bumped Valerie into the water in the process.

"Oh my gosh, I'm so sorry," she called out to Valerie when she resurfaced.

"Help!" Valerie screamed. "I can't swim."

"Stand up," Journee called to her.

"I can't; my heels are sinking into the sand." She flailed around, her movements pronounced and dramatic in the shallow water.

"Seriously? If you can't stand up, then sit down and take off your shoes."

Even from a distance, Grace could hear the disgust in Journee's voice. She didn't want to get involved, but she felt she had no choice since Valerie was technically her guest. With a sigh, she got up and headed for the pier. Before she could get there, Anita came rushing past, screaming at the top of her lungs.

"My baby!" she yelled as she jumped into the water with Valerie. When she realized the water only went up to her calves, she stopped screaming and tried to help Valerie take her heels off, knocking her over and back under the water.

"Ladies," Grace yelled to get their attention. "Anita, there's a ladder on the front of the pier; if you walk over to it, you can climb up and get out of the water."

"What about me?" Valerie whined.

"Sit down and remove your shoes; then you can do the same thing."

"It's too cold," Valerie cried. "Can't you just get me out of here?"

"Valerie, I need you to help me help you, okay?" Grace said, as patient as a saint. "The sooner you get those shoes off, the sooner you can get out of there and to the warm blanket Wyatt has waiting for you."

Wyatt, who must have run track as a teenager, appeared by Grace's side, warm blanket in hand. "I have a blanket, a warm change of clothes, and a bottle of wine with your name on it if you come out of there," he called to her.

That last part perked her up as she finally sat down and removed her shoes. Less than a minute later, she was out of the water and on her way back to the barn to dry off and change her clothes. The drama was finally over; everyone returned to their seats so the wine tasting could continue.

Several hours later, it was time to return home, the wine tasting more or less a success. Valerie and Anita, now wearing sweatsuits with the winery's logo on them, had proceeded to drink their fill of wine and were now singing songs from the eighties at the top of their lungs—a minor improvement over their usual discourse. The rest of the group was either singing along or lost in their own world, yet they seemed happy and relaxed, which was all Grace could ask for at this point.

Back at home, they went their separate ways, the guests going to their rooms while Grace went to the kitchen to start dinner. Luckily for her, she had planned accordingly and already had a roast in the crockpot and sides ready to heat and serve.

"I owe you an apology," Journee said from the door.

"Valerie's the one who ended up in the water," Grace replied.

"She deserved it; you, however, did not. I have a feeling I've only made things worse for you."

"I'm not that worried about it," Grace shrugged. "I am concerned that she might try to retaliate, though. She doesn't seem like the kind of person to let something like that go."

"I suppose I should have thought about that before I 'accidentally' knocked her into the water. Oh well, should make for an entertaining couple of days."

Grace shook her head. "I don't understand how people are okay with that. The smallest hint of anger or confrontation causes me an unending amount of stress and anxiety."

"You must have grown up an only child," she grinned. "My siblings and I lived for fighting and mischief."

"Guilty as charged," Grace said with a laugh. "Hopefully, the two of you can get along from now on."

"Now you sound like my mother!" she teased. "Regardless, don't stress over it, okay? I can handle Valerie and whatever she throws my way."

"I think the real question is, can she handle you?"

Journee gave her a cat-that-ate-the-canary grin, then turned around to go back upstairs, leaving Grace to shake her head in disbelief. At the very least, this would be a memorable experience for her guests. At the worst, it would be a memory they hoped to forget.

-Four-

The day had started out like any other. She had gone to the ranch and done her chores, started breakfast, and then, without warning, chaos erupted. As the guests sat at the dining room table, a shrill scream broke the silence, followed closely by thunder on the stairs.

All eyes now on the doorway, Journee burst through, holding a shampoo bottle in one hand and a clump of what looked like hair in the other. "YOU," she screamed when she saw Valerie. "You did this to me!" She lunged at Valerie, who ducked out of the way and ran around the table in the opposite direction.

They chased each other for a few minutes as everyone stared in stunned silence. Finally, Grace managed to shake off her shock and did her best to intervene. "Ladies," she yelled sharply. When Grace saw she had their attention, she stepped forward between them. "What is going on?" she asked Journee.

"Someone, and by someone, I mean her," she said, pointing to Valerie. "Put hair removal cream in my shampoo bottle." She held up the hand clutching the clump of hair. "My hair is ruined," she cried.

Grace looked at Valerie. "Is this true?"

"You can't prove anything," she spat. "Anyone here could have done it."

"Yeah, but you're the only one who had reason to," Journee protested.

"And why is that, huh? You shoved me into the lake; as far as I'm concerned, you got what you deserved."

"I can't believe you," Journee said as she shook her head. "You ruined my hair all because you got a little wet. What kind of psychopath does something like that?"

"Got a little wet?" Valerie seethed. "You ruined my nine-hundred-dollar Louboutins!"

"Pfft," she sputtered. "They were probably fakes, and even if they weren't, how was I supposed to know they cost that much? They looked like run-of-the-mill shoes to me."

Valerie lunged at Journee, and Grace had to physically hold her back. "THEY HAD RED SOLES!" she screamed. "Everyone knows that only Louboutins have red soles. I'm not the psychopath; you are!"

Grace looked at Rebekah and Molly, who were still seated at the bar. "Do you two think you can handle things here?"

"Of course," they said in unison.

"Great. I'm going to take Journee down to see Evie. Maybe she can find a way to fix this." She turned to Valerie and sighed. "Please try to stay out of trouble while I'm gone."

Valerie sneered, then stomped back to her seat. Choosing to believe that was her way of agreeing, Grace grabbed Journee by the arm and guided her to the door.

"My friend Evie is a professional hair stylist. If anyone can help, it's her."

***

Five minutes later, they walked into Evie's hair salon, The Cutting Edge. "Hey Evie," Grace called out. "We need your help."

Evie took one look at Journee and winced. "What happened?"

Journee held up the bottle. "Someone put hair removal cream in my shampoo bottle. Didn't notice until it was too late."

"Oh wow. What a cruel prank. Come sit down, and we'll see what we can do."

Grace sat down in an empty chair next to Journee. As Evie worked, she saw a flash out of the corner of her eye and, upon further inspection, saw a ring on the tell-tale finger. "Oh my gosh," Grace gasped. "Did Jake propose?"

Evie smiled as she held out her hand for closer inspection. "Yep, just last Saturday. He got permission from Cole to close the bar early and then lured me down there under the pretense of needing help. As soon as I showed up, he had a bottle of champagne, our favorite song on the radio, and a table for two decorated with roses all ready to go."

"That's so romantic," Grace said wistfully. "You must have been so surprised."

"Oh, definitely. We'd talked about getting married, of course, but it was always in the future, ya know?"

Oh boy, did she know. Grace had spent her entire life waiting for 'the future.' That elusive time when everything good was supposed to happen, yet never seemed to materialize. It was difficult not to be jealous, but after everything Evie had been through, she really was happy for her.

"When's the wedding?" asked Journee.

"We decided to get married on the one-year anniversary of our official first date, so in a couple of months."

"That's not much time to plan a wedding," Grace replied.

"We're going to elope," Evie stated matter-of-factly.

Grace nodded in understanding. If she were honest, what happened to Evie during her first wedding was enough to make Grace want to elope. In fact, it might have been enough to make her reconsider getting married at all. Luckily, her friend didn't seem to be having that problem. Something she was glad of. Evie didn't deserve to spend the rest of her life paying for someone else's sins.

"We can throw a celebration party or something after you make it official."

"That would be lovely. Jake and I have talked about inviting everyone over to the cabin sometime. It's small, but the view is incredible and would make an awesome backdrop for a party."

Evie moved Journee over to the hair dryer and got her situated.

"Do you think her hair is going to be okay?" Grace asked in concern.

"Oh yeah. I had to work a little magic, but I'm confident you won't be able to tell once it's dry."

"You're a miracle worker!" Grace enthused.

"I don't know about that," she chuckled. "Luckily, these hair removers are pretty lacking when it comes to quality. Otherwise, this could have been a whole lot worse."

"I know, right? I've tried several of them on my legs, but they never worked. I always figured I must have been doing something wrong since they seem to get rave reviews."

"It's not just you," she laughed. "Anyway, let's see how she looks." She removed the hair dryer, led Journee back to the chair, and handed her a mirror, positioning her so that she could see all angles. "What do you think?"

"It's amazing," she gushed. "I look better than I did before."

"I'm glad you think so," Evie said with a smile. "The short hair suits you."

"I agree," Grace chimed in. "I would never have the guts to go that short, but you look fabulous!"

"Thanks, guys," she grinned. "Wait till Valerie sees me. She will be so disappointed to see that her little plan failed."

"You're probably right. But don't you think it's time for a truce? I shudder to think of what she'll try next."

"I suppose," Journee agreed, although she looked disappointed.

They paid Evie and left her a huge tip.

"Congratulations on your engagement," Journee said on her way out the door. "He's a lucky man."

"I'm really happy for you," Grace said with as big a smile as she could muster.

"Don't worry; I'll do a bouquet toss at the party and make sure it lands in your direction."

"I'm sure I'll have plenty of competition," Grace said, her smile more genuine this time. "Especially from Cassie. It hasn't been very long, but she and Conor seem pretty serious."

"I wouldn't worry about her," Evie waved her hand in dismissal. "For some reason, she has sworn off marriage forever. So she'll either stick to that or shock us all by secretly eloping in Vegas or something. Either way, I can't see her fighting for the bouquet."

"Stranger things have happened."

"That they have. Good luck with whatever you've got going on. Sounds like some serious rivalry if it's gotten to this point."

"Thanks. I'm going to need it. These people are crazy, and I still have six days to go until they leave."

She waved goodbye and made her way back to the car and Journee, who was waiting patiently in the passenger seat. Back at the house, she found Molly and Rebekah in the kitchen discussing some kind of social media campaign.

"How'd it go?" asked Molly, looking up from her computer.

"Well enough. Evie managed to save the day, so another crisis has been averted. Do I even want to know where Valerie is?"

"Last I checked, she's upstairs with Anita, likely plotting something, but she's at least doing it quietly," Rebekah responded.

"Please tell me you have an activity planned for today?" Grace asked hopefully.

"They're going to a cake decorating class with Bea after lunch. It won't keep them occupied for too long, but it's better than nothing," said Molly.

Grace nodded, then wandered over to the game cabinet to peruse the games she had purchased. In the past, her guests had loved game nights—especially ones where they divided up into teams. So tonight, after dinner, she would host a game night. That settled, she went upstairs to start cleaning. Maybe if she were lucky, she would "accidentally" overhear Valerie discussing her evil plan in all its gory details. That's how it goes in the movies, right?

***

It was eleven o'clock, and Grace couldn't sleep. Not because she wasn't tired, oh no, she was exhausted; game night had been a success, but at the cost of her sanity. Valerie and Journee had insisted on being the team captains and had turned the competition into something fierce. There were times Grace had felt more like a referee at a women's battle royale than a pictionary host, but everyone seemed to be having fun, so hey, what do you do? No, the reason she couldn't sleep was because her mind was too unsettled.

Sure Cole was already asleep, she decided to text him a simple, I love you. It wasn't much, but she hadn't seen him in days and hoped it would help relieve some of her loneliness. It wasn't that long ago that he had spent his nights at her house. They'd spent most of their time sleeping, but it had been better than not seeing him at all.

Her phone dinged, and she looked at it in surprise; he was awake after all. Now that she didn't have to worry about waking him up, she dialed his number. "Hey," she said when he answered.

"Hey yourself. Everything alright?"

"No, I miss you, and you aren't here to hold me."

Cole's chuckle sounded in her ear. "You could always sneak over here."

"And risk running into Riley? No thanks, I could live forever without that brand of awkwardness."

"It will only be till the end of the month," Cole assured her.

"Oh no, why? He's not quitting, is he?" She was horrified at the thought. Without Riley's help, she would never see Cole. There was just too much work to do for one person.

"He's moving into Ray and Dot's old house. It seems he's serious about sticking around long-term. And we might have Rebekah to thank for that."

"What about Conor? He just moved in last week. Is he leaving?"

"There is a bit of shuffling around going on among our friends. Evie is moving into Jake's cabin, and Conor and Cassie are moving to Hope Springs and in with Emilio and Vanessa."

"They're already moving in together?" Grace asked in surprise.

"Vanessa and Cassie are going to live in one side of the duplex while Conor and Emilio live in the other," he explained.

"That makes sense. I wish we lived together," she said wistfully.

It took a moment for him to answer, making her heart tense in concern. "Me too, but it's better this way—for now, at least. We'll see how things go once your latest batch of guests leave."

"You mean Valerie," she rolled her eyes.

"Yes, I mean Valerie. I imagine part of her plan included running into me in the middle of the night. I would rather not give her the satisfaction nor the opportunity to cause any more problems than she already has."

"Fine," Grace said in frustration. Yes, she agreed with him, but that didn't mean she had to like it. It sucked that this woman had so much power over their lives. Would things ever return to normal? Or would she spend the rest of her life at the mercy of others?

"I'll be there in ten minutes. Make sure you're outside waiting so we don't accidentally wake the she-beast."

Grace laughed as she hung up the phone. It wasn't the nicest description in the world, but it was fitting after the stunt Valerie pulled earlier that day. She threw some clothes on and rushed downstairs, anxious to see Cole. When he pulled up to the curb, she jumped in the truck and threw her arms around his neck.

"Hello to you too," he laughed.

"I missed you," she said sheepishly.

"I missed you, too." He put his arm around her and pulled away from the curb.

"Where are we going?"

"You'll see."

A few minutes later, they pulled up to the gate of one of his field accesses. He got out to unlock the gate while she pulled the truck through so he could shut it after her. Back in the truck, he drove them over to a copse of trees and then got out. Grace followed him, curious as to what he was doing. He had never brought her out into the field in the middle of the night before.

"Hop in," he said, lowering the tailgate.

She did as she was told and found that he had already spread out a bunch of pillows and blankets, turning the back of his truck into a makeshift bed. Lifting the top blanket, she slid underneath and waited for him to join her.

"It's not the Ritz-Carlton, but hopefully, it'll do." He slid in beside her and pulled her into his arms.

"It's perfect," she replied dreamily. The sky above them was clear, the stars in full view. It was the sweetest and the most romantic thing he had ever done for her. She could easily spend the rest of her life in the back of the truck as long as he was with her.

He kissed her forehead. "I love you, babe."

"I love you, too." This time, when she closed her eyes, she fell asleep dreaming of him.

-Three-

T he following day, Cole dropped Grace off at the barn with a promise to see her later that night. As he drove off, Rebekah pulled up in Grace's car. "Hope you don't mind," she said, nodding toward the vehicle.

"Not at all," Grace replied. "I'll admit I didn't expect to see you this morning."

Rebekah shrugged. "It didn't seem right to weasel out of coming if I still had a way to get here."

"I appreciate that, but helping isn't a requirement."

"Yeah, I know, but it's been good for me. For the first time in my life, I'm doing something that actually serves a purpose. In fact, I was wondering if there might be more ways I can help?"

Grace raised her brow. "What did you have in mind?"

"Well..." Rebekah trailed off, a hint of nervousness in her voice.

Surprised to see the usually confident woman struggle with her words, Grace waited patiently, sure that whatever she had to say would be worth it. When a full minute passed and Rebekah was still silent, Grace prompted her. "What happened to the woman that demanded exotic desserts, knowing full well the ingredients were impossible to get?" Grace teased.

"Her parents cut her off financially, leaving her dead broke and at the mercy of the woman she previously abused," she deadpanned.

"I take it you've heard from your parents?" She tried to ask gently, but the topic made it difficult.

"They called me last night. Said if I wasn't on the next plane to New York, they would cancel my credit cards and permanently close my bank accounts first thing this morning. No second chances."

"I'm sorry." Grace reached over and squeezed her hand. "I can't imagine how you must be feeling right now."

Rebekah looked up at Grace, her eyes full of pain. "It's not just losing the money. It's knowing their love is conditional and so easy for them to take away. You have no idea how lucky you are to have your granny." She looked away, but not before Grace saw the tears in her eyes.

"What can I do to help?"

"I need a place to stay while I try to figure out how to support myself. I know one of the rooms upstairs is smaller than the rest, so I was wondering if you would let me stay in that room in exchange for cooking and cleaning. And, of course, helping out here." She took a deep breath. "To be honest, I have never had to cook or clean before, so you'll have to teach me, but I'm willing to learn."

"Deal."

"Really?" She looked up at Grace, equal parts shocked and relieved. "Just like that?"

Grace shrugged. "Just like that. Now, we should probably get a move on here. I have a fun day planned for everyone."

Rebekah hugged her. "Thank you so much!"

As they were finishing up the morning chores, Riley came by and stopped to talk. "Hey, ladies," he said casually.

"Hey," Grace replied. She turned to Rebekah. "I need to make a phone call. I'll wait for you in the car, okay?"

She nodded and handed Grace the keys. "I won't be long."

Sadly, Cole was nowhere to be found, but Grace already knew to expect that. It didn't stop her from looking, though, just in case. She didn't have a phone call to make either; she just wanted to give Rebekah and Riley some time alone. Whether or not they had a future together remained to be seen, but Grace felt they could be good for each other. Starting over was not easy, and it helped to have support from someone who understands what you're going through. Back in the car, Rebekah was giddy as a schoolgirl. "Riley asked me out," she said by way of explanation.

"That's great," Grace replied enthusiastically. "When's the big date?"

"Tonight. He said Cole gave him the night off."

Grace nodded. "Cole and I are supposed to go out as well."

"Oh, should we do a double?"

"A double?" Grace asked, her brow furrowed in confusion.

"You know, a double date."

"Are you sure you want to do that? It doesn't sound like you'll have a lot of privacy if Cole and I are tagging along."

"You mean, you two won't have a lot of privacy," Rebekah wiggled her eyebrows, causing Grace to laugh.

"If you don't think it's a big deal, then sure, it sounds fun."

Rebekah was silent the rest of the way home. When they parked in the driveway, she turned to Grace with a concerned expression. "What should I wear?"

"Um." Was this a trick question? Rebekah was the queen of fashion; if anything, Grace should be asking her that question, not the other way around.

"I'm not used to dating cowboys," she explained. "I don't want him to think I'm some kind of uppity New Yorker, you know?"

"I think I understand what you mean," Grace said slowly. "You want him to like you for you, though. So wear something you feel comfortable in."

"Like yoga pants and a T-shirt?" She looked uncertain.

"No, like an outfit you would feel comfortable wearing to a restaurant. If you would feel more natural in a summer dress than jeans and cowboy boots, you should wear the summer dress."

"Okay." She still looked uncertain, but a little less so.

They went inside to shower and change and then met back in the kitchen to make breakfast. Rebekah insisted on helping, despite Grace reminding her she was still officially a guest until Monday. Apparently, people really could change. If you had asked Grace even one week ago if she could imagine Rebekah cooking and cleaning, she would have laughed you out of town. Yet, here she was, doing her best to learn how to make cinnamon rolls and muffins. It would have been so easy to return to New York and the life she'd always known. The fact that she refused, despite the consequences, gave Grace a newfound respect for her.

Once the rest of the guests were seated at the table, Grace made the big announcement. "Today, we're doing something entertaining." She waited until she had everyone's attention. "We're going on a scavenger hunt up in the city!"

Only a few people looked interested; the rest stared at her blankly. "It's a competition," she tried again to stir some excitement, "with prizes in the form of gift cards to local businesses." They perked up at the mention of gift cards.

"How many teams?" asked Valerie. She attempted to look bored, but it was apparent from her tone of voice that she was more than a little interested.

"Two teams, and I figured, in the interest of saving time, that we could use the same teams from the game night if everyone agrees?" She looked around the room and inwardly sighed in relief when everyone agreed. The first time they had chosen teams had been a nightmare, and Grace had no desire to experience round two. "Great. Once breakfast is done, we can load the bus and be on our way."

***

The scavenger hunt had Grace questioning everything she had ever done in her life since she must have done something horrible to deserve her current fate. Valerie and Journee had led their respective teams through the most grueling gauntlet of a scavenger hunt ever known to humankind. Unfortunately, both of them were so determined to win, what should have been a multiple-hour, fun sightseeing adventure was reduced to a forty-five-minute marathon full of complaining, sore feet, and more than a few threats to quit from their teammates.

Also unfortunately for them, to win, their entire team had to complete the challenge. By the time they finished, no one was talking to anyone else, and everyone was hot, sweaty, and disgruntled. Valerie, to her credit, had won, but to be fair, her team consisted of Anita and the two young girls, Izzie and Violet.

Journee's team included Julie, Kate, and Stella. Since Grace was from the area, she had chosen to sit this out due to an unfair advantage, and Rebekah joined her to make the teams even. Not that it mattered, since they chased the others through the city and were just as hot and tired as everyone else.

To ease the tension, Grace had taken everyone to the food court at the local mall, where they could eat and do some shopping. By the time they were ready to return home, moods had improved, and for the most part, they were once again getting along. Well, as much as they had been before the scavenger hunt.

Before they could leave for their date, Grace and Rebekah had to get dinner ready, Grace having promised

Molly to have it done before she took over hosting duties for the evening. Grace had no idea what Molly planned to do to entertain them for the evening, but she hoped she had better luck than Grace had with the scavenger hunt. Regardless, she was going to have her hands full.

Rebekah and Grace met Cole and Riley at Cole's house; Grace was too afraid of Valerie pulling a stunt if Cole showed his face anywhere near her. They decided to take Cole's truck to the new French restaurant in the city, Grace and Cole in the front seat, Rebekah and Riley in the back. If that sounds awkward, well, it was. She felt like a chaperone for a couple of teenagers and did her best to keep the group entertained with stories from earlier in the day while everyone else sat quietly listening, or not, to her talk. Eventually, she gave up, and they spent the rest of the trip in silence.

The restaurant was nice but had a 'chain' feel, much like a 'certain' Italian restaurant famous for its endless breadsticks. When she saw the prices on the menu, she almost had a heart attack. Yes, there was a surprising amount of pasta options for a French restaurant, but they were two to three times the amount of money they would have cost at that 'other' restaurant. The steak and seafood options were even worse. This meal was going to cost more than her utility bills.

A glance across the table showed Rebekah faring even worse. Grace had zero doubt in her mind that restaurants like these had been a common occurrence for Rebekah, but that was before she had been cut off. Now that she was responsible for paying her way, things looked a little different. She glanced up at Grace, her eyes wide with concern, and for the second time since she'd met her, Grace truly felt sorry for her.

As if sensing their panic, Cole spoke up. "Order whatever you want, everyone; dinner's on me." He squeezed Grace's knee under the table, confirming her belief he had picked up on their distress.

She smiled in response but spent a long time scouring the menu for the cheapest option. When the waiter returned to take their order, it appeared that Rebekah had done the same, as their orders were identical.

"I figured you for a lobster kind of girl," Riley teased Rebekah.

"I'm not a big fan of shellfish," she replied.

Grace was pretty sure that wasn't true; Rebekah had eaten her share of crab puffs last Valentine's Day, but she wasn't about to call her out. "I'm working on the menu for Mother's Day this Sunday," she said to change the topic. "Anyone have any suggestions? I'd like it to be special, but maybe not 'this' special." She waved her hand around to indicate the restaurant.

"In my opinion, you can never go wrong with a good steak," said Riley.

"If you do steaks, we can grill them, which will save you some work," Cole put his arm around her shoulders and pulled her close. "Knowing you, you'll have a ton of side dishes and desserts to go with it."

"We?" she asked in surprise. "Aren't you avoiding the B&B right now?"

"Oh no, I'm looking forward to the big showdown between you and Valerie when her lies about my 'mother' are exposed."

"I was hoping to avoid having that confrontation in front of the rest of my guests," Grace rolled her eyes. "It would be entertaining to see their reaction if you showed up, though. Might be worth the potential fireworks."

"You won't get any complaints from Journee," said Rebekah. "She would love nothing more than to see Valerie get her comeuppance. Especially after her brutal loss earlier today."

"Oh yeah, Journee would definitely cheer from the sidelines. It's Kate and Stella I'm worried about. They don't seem like the type to appreciate all this drama, and they've already gotten more than their fair share."

"I wouldn't worry about it too much," said Cole. "As long as your guests are having a good time, they'll overlook the crazy."

Grace wasn't so sure about that, but she didn't want to waste any more of their evening talking about Valerie. They spent the rest of the night talking and laughing; the food, despite its cost—or maybe because of it—was a highlight of the night. From where she sat, Rebekah and Riley seemed to be hitting it off, their first-date awkwardness wearing off as the night went on.

When they got home, Grace and Cole walked through the field to give them some privacy. "Thank you for dinner," Grace looked up at him shyly.

"You're welcome." He leaned down and kissed her on the nose. "I had a lot of fun tonight."

"You sound surprised."

"I knew I would have a good time with you; it was the other two I was worried about. Especially Rebekah. She's changed, hasn't she?"

Grace nodded. "She's been through a lot lately. I agreed to let her move in with me."

Cole whistled. "Are you sure about that? It wasn't that long ago you were kicking her out, and she was only a guest then."

"Trust me; the irony has not escaped my notice. But she has nowhere to go. And, as you said, she's changed. Everyone deserves a second chance."

He stopped walking and pulled her into his arms. "You're a good person, Grace."

"Thank you, but I'm only doing what everyone else would do."

"You're wrong about that." He kissed her deeply, trying to show her how he felt about her. When he ended the kiss, he whispered in her ear. "I love you."

"I love you, too," she whispered back. "I guess I better go. Rebekah is waiting for me to take her home."

"And if I came by later to pick you up again like last night?"

"I would be waiting with open arms."

"Then I'll see you later." He kissed her again and then led her back to her car, where Rebekah was indeed waiting. "Twenty minutes," he whispered.

Grace smiled and nodded, then got in the car. Twenty minutes felt like a lifetime, but he was worth the wait.

Days till Mother's Day

-Two-

Molly was waiting in the dining room when Grace and Rebekah returned from their early morning trip to the ranch. "Good morning," said Grace. "Is everything okay?"

"Yeah," Molly sighed. "The tired phase is over and has been replaced with the I'm-uncomfortable-and-can't-sleep phase."

"How far along are you?" asked Rebekah.

"About nineteen weeks," Molly counted on her fingers. "So, around five months. I can't wait until this little guy or girl gets here. I'm already over being pregnant."

"Molly isn't known for her patience," Grace teased. She pulled out ingredients for hash browns, sausage, and homemade waffles.

"No, I'm not," Molly agreed. "But just wait till you're in my shoes; trust me, you'll feel the same way."

"I imagine it'll be a while before that happens. For both of us," she said, looking at Rebekah.

"Speaking of which, how did the big date go last night?"

Rebekah blushed and looked away. "Um, it went well, I think."

"You think?" asked Molly. "Did he ask you out on a second date?"

"Not exactly. He is planning to come over on Mother's Day, though."

"So, your next date is the barbecue on Sunday?" asked Molly. She seemed confused, although, to be fair, so did Rebekah.

"I'm not sure I would call it a date when he was already planning to come with Cole." She sighed. "Honestly, I'm not sure what's going on. I want to go out on a second date, but Riley never mentioned anything official. Just said he would see me Sunday."

"Hmm, maybe someone needs to do some sleuthing," Molly looked at Grace expectantly.

"What would you have me do? Send Riley a note that says, 'Do you like Rebekah? Check yes or no'?"

"Very funny," Molly rolled her eyes. "Obviously, you could ask Cole. I'm sure the two of them talk."

"Fine," Grace sighed.

"You don't have to," said Rebekah. Her cheeks were still red from embarrassment.

Before she could answer, the guests arrived; Valerie and Journee studiously ignored each other. "Good morning, everyone," Grace called out cheerfully.

"What's on the agenda for today?" asked Stella.

As far as Grace could tell, Stella was a reserved woman who only spoke when necessary. The fact she felt the need to question the day's activities made Grace a little nervous. Either she was having a great time and looking forward to the next event, or she was having a terrible time and dreading participating in another activity.

Grace answered with as much excitement as she could muster. "Today is our mother-daughter spa day!"

"What does that consist of?" asked Julie. She eyed Anita and Valerie at the other end of the table.

"I made staggered appointments for you at three different places: Amy's Gentle Touch, Lulu's Hair and Nail Salon, and Chrissy's Boutique, where you will be treated to a massage, a manicure, and a new outfit to wear to the mother-daughter tea party you're going to tomorrow."

"What do you mean by staggered?" Julie was still eyeing Valerie and Anita, her gaze never leaving them.

"I mean, you will be taking turns at each location. One mother-daughter duo per appointment."

"This sounds like a perfect bonding opportunity," Kate said enthusiastically.

"That is certainly my intention," Grace replied warmly. "I have a schedule prepared with the time and locations of each of your appointments." She passed out a sheet of paper to each of the duos.

"What about her?" Valerie pointed to Rebekah. "Her 'mother' left early."

Grace watched her use air quotes on the word 'mother' and wanted to scream. The woman had a lot of nerve to criticize Rebekah when she was lying about her own companion. Especially since Rebekah never lied. "Molly will be filling in for Amelia," Grace replied through gritted teeth. Monday morning couldn't come soon enough.

"I am?" Molly asked from the bar.

Having forgotten she was back there, Grace whipped around to see her looking at her in surprise. "Yes, you are. You're going to be a mother, so it's only fitting." She turned back to face the others before Molly could object. "Now, if there are no more questions, the first appointment starts in one hour. If you need me, text the number on the top of the schedule; I will be in and out for the rest of the day."

That done, she moved back to the kitchen to start cleaning up the breakfast dishes and put some distance between her and the guests. Playing hostess was exhausting. More so when you added unwelcome guests to the list of people she had to entertain.

"You should go with Rebekah," Molly whispered. "If anyone needs a relaxing day, it's you."

"I have too much to do," Grace replied. "Besides, Rebekah could use a little guidance right now, and who better to give it than the marketing master!"

"You want me to give her career advice over manicures and a massage?"

Grace shrugged. "Whatever you think will help. Since I know how much you love marketing, I figure this will be right up your alley."

"Well, I do love marketing," she said thoughtfully. "Alright, if you insist. Once this is over, though, you're going to have your own 'spa day.'"

"If there's time. Grant told me the hotel deal is back on the table. If it goes through, we'll have a very busy summer ahead of us."

"I suppose that's true. Even still, we'll make time. You and Granny could use some time together to bond."

The idea held some appeal, but she had too much to do to worry about it right now. Once the guests finished eating, she cleared the table, put the dishes in the dishwasher, and then got to work on her grocery list. She had stocked up on groceries the other day, but she still needed steaks and a few other ingredients for some last-minute Sunday menu additions. Since it was Mother's Day, she wanted it to be as memorable as possible.

In addition to the food, she planned to have flowers delivered to the guests and had made each of them a framed picture to take home with them of one of the memories they had created while they were here. She'd even made one for Valerie and Anita, despite having no idea who Anita was—though she did have her suspicions.

As the hour approached, Grace looked for Izzie and found her playing with Piper and Ruby in the living room. "Can I talk to you for a minute?" she asked as she sat on the floor next to the teen.

Izzie looked up at her from beneath hooded eyes. "What's up?"

"I know it's none of my business, and I have no idea what your relationship with your mom has been like the last seventeen years, but she does seem to be trying, and I'm hoping you'll be open to giving her a chance."

"She's had seventeen years to try; what makes this time so special?"

"Time is running out."

Izzie raised a brow. "What does that mean? Is she sick or something?"

"No, nothing like that," Grace rushed to assure her. "But, you will be going off to college soon. She's worried that she'll lose you forever if she doesn't do something to change things now."

"Maybe she should have thought about that all those years she chose to put her career ahead of me."

This was not going well. Grace was woefully unqualified to be sticking her nose in other people's business, yet she still seemed to do it every single time. "Look, I'm not trying to lay a guilt trip on you. You have absolutely every right to feel the way you do; it's just—parents are people too, and they make mistakes just like everyone else. Your mom knows she messed up and is trying to fix things. Not everyone is willing to admit when they're wrong, let alone try to make it right."

"If you were me, would you forgive your mom?"

Grace sucked in a breath at the thought of her mom. "I can't answer that, Izzie. My mom died when I was five, so obviously, I would give everything I have for another chance to be with her. But that isn't fair to you. So I will say that life is short, and holding on to pain and sadness hurts you as much as it does the person who caused it—sometimes more."

"Izzie?" Kate popped her head into the living room. "Are you ready to go?"

"Yeah." She stood up and handed Piper to Grace. "I'll think about what you said," she told Grace. "No promises."

"That's enough for me. Have fun, you two!" she smiled at them both, ignoring the question in Kate's eyes. She truly hoped the two would find a way to patch things up and forge a strong bond moving forward.

***

As far as she could tell, the day had been a huge success. The guests had spent the day at their activities, including lunch at Addie's and dessert at Bea's Bakery, giving Grace more than enough time to get her shopping done. All of them, including Valerie and Anita, had returned to the B&B happy and relaxed.

Dinner that night was a Mexican-themed buffet the guests were invited to attend at their leisure, allowing Grace to skip out early to spend time with Cole. When she arrived at the ranch, she found him saddling up a couple of horses in the barn. "I thought we'd go for a ride," he said by way of greeting.

"Sounds good to me," she replied. She waited until he was done and hoisted herself into the saddle. "Where to?"

"Wherever they take us," he shrugged.

"Lead the way."

They rode for ten minutes before the horses stopped by the pond for a drink of water. When Cole dismounted, she did the same and followed him over to a tree-lined clearing, where she discovered a blanket and picnic basket waiting. "Wherever they take us?" she raised her brow.

Cole grinned. "I might have guided them a little," he said, putting his thumb and forefinger together.

It was warm in the sun but cool in the shade, which made the little clearing the perfect spot for a picnic. "Thanks for doing this," she gestured to the blanket and basket, which she discovered contained a bottle of wine and one of Bea's famous strawberry shortcakes. Her eyes lit up on the latter; it had been a while since she'd had the seasonal dessert.

"Bea made it just for you," he explained.

"That was awfully sweet of her. And you," she kissed him, humbled by his thoughtfulness.

"It was the least I could do after what you've been through this past week," he replied.

"You are not responsible for Valerie's schemes," she reminded him.

"No, but she wouldn't bother you if it wasn't for me."

"Maybe not, but that still doesn't make it your fault. I'll still accept the shortcake, though."

He laughed as he fed her a bite. "I would expect nothing less." They ate in silence for a couple of minutes. "How are things going with Rebekah?"

"Pretty well. She's been helping out as promised and has proven to be an ally where Valerie's concerned, so..." she trailed off as she remembered her earlier conversation with Molly and Rebekah. "Speaking of Rebekah, what do you think about her and Riley?"

"What about them?"

"You know, their relationship?"

"No, I don't know. I was under the impression they'd only gone on one date, and that date was with us. Grace, stop beating around the bush and ask your question already."

Grace rolled her eyes and sighed. "Am I that obvious?"

"Yes," he licked the whipped cream off her nose, then sat back on his forearms and looked at her expectantly.

"Some of us are wondering if you know how Riley feels about Rebekah, as in, is he interested in dating her?"

"Even though we live and work together, we don't spend much time together," he replied. "We're pretty much ships passing in the night while we rush to get the fields planted."

"So you have no idea how he feels about her?"

"He was interested enough to ask her out," he shrugged.

"Yeah, but he didn't ask her out on a second date; he just said he'd see her Sunday."

"Ah, I see where the confusion is coming from. As far as I know, Riley thinks Rebekah is just another one of your guests, meaning he thinks she'll be leaving on Monday."

"He doesn't want to get involved with a woman he thinks is leaving in a few days," Grace stated.

"Would you?" he winced once the words were out of his mouth.

Grace knew what he was thinking. That was precisely what she had done with Hunter when he stayed at the B&B during Christmas. "It's alright," she assured him. "I know you didn't mean it like that."

"No, I didn't. I just meant that Riley wants to put down some roots and is looking for someone he can do that with."

"Rebekah plans to stay, you know."

"For now, maybe. But what about the long term? Has she said anything about that?"

"I guess not," she replied after taking a few minutes to think about it. Rebekah was in survival mode, her focus on taking care of her immediate needs. Beyond that, she didn't have a plan, and Grace was foolish to assume that her future was in Winterwood.

"Hey," he lifted her chin to look her in the eyes. "I didn't bring you out here to worry about Rebekah and Riley. They can take care of themselves, okay?"

"You're right," she sighed. She had a bad habit of worrying about things out of her control while missing out on what was right in front of her. Such as a much-needed opportunity to spend time with her boyfriend. "How about we focus on us instead?"

He pulled her into his arms and kissed her. "I like the sound of that," he whispered in her ear.

Seconds later, she forgot about everything but Cole.

-One-

"I talked to Cole," Grace said casually as she prepared breakfast. Two pairs of eyes were immediately on her. "Riley thinks you're planning to skip town on Monday, so he's keeping his distance."

"Then why bother to ask me out in the first place?"

"That I cannot answer. My best guess is he likes you and couldn't help himself."

"Aww, that's sweet," said Molly.

The two of them were sitting at the bar chopping fruit while Grace made the batter for the crepes she was serving for breakfast. "If that's not your plan, you might want to make sure he gets the memo."

Molly made a face. "Word down at town hall is that Katie has her eye on him."

"Who's Katie?" asked Rebekah.

"She's the town manager," Grace explained. "If you look up the word 'spirited' in the dictionary, you'll see her picture."

"Is that a nice way of saying she's high-strung?" Molly said with a laugh.

"Well, she is. But she's one of the nicest people you'll ever meet," Grace added quickly.

"Should I be worried about her?" asked Rebekah.

Grace wasn't sure how to answer that. She had no idea how Riley felt about anything, much less two very different women. "You should talk to Riley and clear up any misconceptions he might have," Grace hedged. "If there are misconceptions?"

"What do you mean?"

"I mean, you haven't exactly come up with a plan yet. Do you intend to be here past Monday?"

Rebekah looked down at her lap, her face unreadable. "Are you still willing to let me stay in exchange for cooking and cleaning?"

She sounded so hopeful that, for the first time, Grace truly understood just how scared and alone she felt. "Of course," she replied. "You can stay as long as you want. I just wasn't sure that you wanted to. Winterwood is a far cry from New York City."

"I don't ever want to go back there again," she said vehemently. "Every bad memory I have happened there." She began to chop the fruit with a little more force than necessary.

Seeing her distress, Grace decided to change the subject. "Are you two ready for the tea room?"

"Yes, although I wish you were going," Molly replied. She was giving Rebekah the side-eye as she continued to viciously chop fruit.

"I'm afraid Cinderella will have to skip this particular ball," replied Grace. "Someone has to get the food ready for tomorrow. Besides, Granny and Gladys claim the trip is too much for them, so someone needs to stay here with them."

"I'll stay, too," Rebekah put the knife down, her fruit closer to a compote than fruit slices. "I promised to help with the cooking."

"I appreciate that, but you are still a guest and deserve to go. We can worry about the cooking and cleaning next week." She did not look convinced.

"Good morning," Journee said, her voice overly cheerful.

Grace handed her a cup of coffee. "What did Valerie do now?"

"Somehow," she drawled out the word, "a snake managed to find its way into my bed last night."

Horrified, Grace stepped back, her hand going to her chest. "Oh my gosh, are you okay?"

"It was just a garden snake," Journee shrugged. "Regardless, I did not appreciate the uninvited guest."

"That's it!" Grace exclaimed. "It's time for her to go. I don't care if they sue me or film me or whatever they have planned. This is too much." She marched toward the stairs, months' worth of pent-up anger boiling to the surface.

Journee grabbed her shoulders and pulled her back. "Don't worry, Grace. I already took care of it."

A scream rent the air, causing an evil grin to spread across Journee's face. "What did you do?"

"I put a slug in her high heel," she replied, a smug smile on her face.

Thunder sounded on the stairs before a visibly shaken Valerie burst into the room. "You," she screamed at Journee. She pointed her heel at her. "You did this!"

"Did what?" she asked innocently. She sipped her coffee as if she didn't have a care in the world.

"You put this, this thing in my shoe!"

"I have no idea what you're talking about. Although, now that you mention it, I found something interesting in my bed this morning. You wouldn't happen to know anything about that, would you?"

Valerie opened her mouth to respond, then closed it again, her eyes narrowing in concentration. Grace could see the exact moment her plan fell into place in her mind, a shiver running down her spine as she knew it would involve her.

"According to you," Valerie said slowly, "both of us ended up with vermin in our rooms this morning." She turned and pointed her shoe at Grace. "That must mean that the B&B is infested. Just wait till the rest of the guests hear about this!"

"I never said I found vermin in my room," Journee said, interrupting Valerie's moment of triumph. "The only thing I said was that I found something interesting." She stepped in Valerie's direction, causing the other woman to step back. "Sounds to me like you might be the source of this so-called infestation."

"She's right," Rebekah chimed in, clearly enjoying Valerie's discomfort. "How else would you have known that Journee found vermin in her room unless you're the one that put it there? I wouldn't be surprised if you put the vermin in your shoe as well."

Valerie sputtered out a few curses. "Why would I do that?"

"I can think of several reasons," said Grace. Her voice was full of barely contained rage. "Ruining my reputation and trying to extort a refund is at the top of the list."

The rest of the guests came in with curious expressions on their faces. "What's going on?" asked Violet.

"Valerie is trying to sabotage the B&B," replied Journee. She was still sipping her coffee as she casually leaned against the edge of the bar.

"Seriously?" asked Kate. She looked horrified, her eyes wide as saucers. "Should we be worried?"

"Of course not," Valerie snapped. "There's simply been a misunderstanding, that's all." She turned on her heel and stomped back out of the room, leaving them all to stare after her in shock.

"You want to tell us what that was all about?" asked Stella.

"Just more of the same," replied Journee, pointing toward her hair.

The small gesture seemed enough for them to put two and two together, the guests visibly relaxing when they realized the latest drama, once again, had nothing to do with them.

"Crepes?" Grace asked as she held up a plate of mascarpone cheese-stuffed crepes. Luckily for her, the delectable delicacies were enough to distract her guests from Valerie's outburst and onto more pleasant things.

"What time are we leaving today?" asked Stella. She drizzled her crepes with strawberries and whipped cream, then stuffed bite-sized pieces in her mouth.

Grace watched in fascination as the usually reserved woman threw caution to the wind and devoured her breakfast in practically one gulp. "We're supposed to leave around eleven," she replied after giving herself a mental shake.

"See," said Violet. "Plenty of time for a fashion show. I, for one, would love to see the outfits everyone picked out yesterday."

"Sounds good to me," said Grace.

"Then it's settled. As soon as breakfast is over, we'll all get changed and meet back here for a little show."

Grace nodded in agreement with Violet's plan. "I'll get Granny and Gladys so we can be your audience. The stairs would make a good runway, so we will sit at the table."

Violet clapped her hands. "This is going to be so much fun!" She finished her crepes and rushed upstairs to get ready, her mother following at a much more subdued pace.

A few minutes later, Grace was left alone to clean up the breakfast mess, wondering if anyone would tell Valerie and Anita about the fashion show. Usually, it was up to her to ensure everyone was included, but she was still mad about the snake incident. Journee could have been seriously hurt. Was there no low Valerie wouldn't stoop to? Was this the first time she had wondered that?

It turns out Violet was so excited about the show, she had been kind enough to invite Valerie. And, true to form, Valerie had done her utmost to hijack the show and make it all about her, acting as if she were making her debut at New York Fashion Week. Thankfully, she had chosen to go last, likely because, in her mind, that made her the star.

Once that was over, Grace all but shoved them out the door and onto the bus, desperate for some time alone. One could only take so much drama before it became too much, and she reached her tolerance threshold several incidents ago.

What had once been a source of stress had become a source of relaxation. Before Valentine's Day, Grace had been considered a terror in the kitchen, her penchant for burning things legendary among those who knew her. Now, while not quite an expert, after countless hours of trial and error, she was at least a decent cook, her favorite thing to make the custard tart. The tarts were her one claim to fame, her most requested recipe.

She spent hours baking and listening to music while she churned out one recipe after another, the kitchen quickly turning into an assembly line. By the time she was done, instead of feeling a sense of peace and accomplishment, she felt unsettled. Or maybe disgruntled. Either way, she was upset and didn't know what to do about it.

After giving it some thought, she set the ingredients for sub-style sandwiches out on the bar, made a couple for Cole, and then drove to his house. It was still early, for him at least, so it was no surprise that he wasn't there when she arrived. So, she grabbed her stuff, tossed it on the seat next to her, and took off in the side-by-side farm vehicle to find him.

It took several minutes to drive from Cole's ranch to the fields and then several more to figure out which tractor was his and make her way over to him. Finally, she parked on the side of the field and waited for him to make his way to her. It was a long wait, but it gave her time to think.

When he reached the edge, he shut down the tractor and climbed into the side-by-side beside her. "You're a sight for sore eyes," he said as he kissed her. "What's wrong?"

"What makes you think something's wrong?" she asked as she handed him one of the sandwiches she made for him.

Cole rolled his eyes as he accepted the sandwich. "Baby, I love you, but I don't have time for guessing games."

"I know I came here to talk to you, but now that I see how much work you have to do, I feel bad that I interrupted."

"I told you I would always make time for you, remember?"

"Yeah, but it feels more like I'm wasting your time." Grace took a deep breath and sighed. "I don't know what's wrong. This time of the year has always been hard for me, as I imagine it is for you," she looked at him with sympathy. "But, it's not just that."

He raised his brow in question but stayed silent as he waited for her to continue.

"The Traditional Christmas Experience had felt so magical, not just because of Hunter," she quickly added. "The whole community was involved, there was snow and decorations, and the guests were all lovely people..." she trailed off as the memories flashed before her eyes. "It was everything I had hoped it would be and then some."

"And all that changed," he said softly. He grabbed her hand and squeezed it, doing his best to be supportive.

"There have been problems every single time since. It doesn't feel magical anymore. It feels exhausting. Like my home is no longer my own."

"I imagine Valerie is playing a big part in that. Rebekah too."

"They certainly aren't helping. It's crazy that I'm stuck with these people in my house when I do not want them there." She looked over at him and saw that his sandwich was gone, so she handed him another one with a bottle of water.

"Thank you," he replied gratefully.

"I'm also jealous of Evie and Jake, and I hate myself for that. They deserve every bit of their happiness."

"But?"

"But I miss you," she turned back to face him. "I know what you're going to say. I lack patience; I'm rushing things, blah blah blah. The truth is, I've known you were the one since the first moment I met you. I'm tired of all this waiting; I just want to be with you."

"Sweetheart, you are with me," he pulled her into his arms and held her tight.

"You know what I mean. I want to go to bed with you each night and wake up next to you each morning. I miss making you coffee before we start the chores and having dinner together and—" she was interrupted by his kiss, a welcome distraction from the anxiety she was causing herself. "I willingly shovel horse poop every morning because the thirty minutes it takes me is worth the ten I get to spend with you," she said when they ended.

"Should we run off to Vegas and get married by Elvis?" he teased.

"I would even be okay with a drive-thru," she replied earnestly.

Cole opened his mouth to respond, but Grace cut him off. "I'm the same age my parents were when they died. Time doesn't mean the same thing to me as it does to others. I've experienced first-hand just how short it can be."

"That's not a reason to rush into a life-long commitment, baby," he said gently. "And marriage is sadly no longer a lifetime guarantee."

"Are you worried I'll turn out to be just like Valerie?" she tried to hide her hurt but couldn't quite pull it off.

"Of course not," he said quickly. "You are nothing like Valerie. That thought has never entered my head."

"Then what is it?"

He stayed silent for so long Grace was sure he wouldn't answer. So she tried to figure out a way to leave without causing a fight when he finally opened his mouth.

"Jake and Evie are getting married on their one-year anniversary. What if we agree to do the same?"

"I don't want to get married around Valentine's Day," Grace pouted. "There are too many bad memories from that time."

"Hmm, okay, how about sometime in March, then?"

"How about Halloween?"

"Okay, I wasn't expecting that one," he said in surprise. "New Year's?"

Grace didn't like that one either. Too many memories of Hunter. "Thanksgiving?"

Cole thought it over and then nodded. "I guess that could work. Why don't we get through the next few days and see how you feel? A lot of these emotions could just be the result of stress."

That wasn't what she wanted to hear, but it was an acceptable compromise for the time being. "Okay, I'll let you get back to work."

"Hey," he pulled her back to him. "Are you going to be okay?"

"Yeah, I'll be fine."

"How about I pick you up again after work? It's still supposed to be cool tonight, and I like sleeping out under the stars with you."

"Text me when you're on your way, and I'll be waiting outside when you arrive."

He took his time kissing her goodbye, neither anxious to leave. Finally, he pulled away and got out of the vehicle. "Thanks again for the sandwiches."

"Thanks for listening," she smiled and waved and then turned around to leave. There were only two more days to go until things would hopefully return to normal. She could handle that, right?

The big day had finally arrived, and not a moment too soon. When Grace had returned home after talking to Cole the night before, she had found Valerie and Journee, once again, at odds, the latter accusing the former of ruining her new outfit. According to Journee and several others who witnessed the 'accident,' Valerie had knocked her teacup over, and the tea had spilled all over Journee's lap. Since she was wearing white pants with blue flowers, she was understandably upset. Of course, that wasn't enough. When they arrived back at the B&B, Journee had attempted to rinse the pants out in the sink, only for Valerie to 'accidentally' spill a glass of wine onto the already stained clothing.

To say that tensions were high would have been an understatement. To stop the women from trying to kill each other, Grace had to call Chrissy's personal cell and convince her to open up her shop long enough for Grace to buy Journee a replacement pair of pants. Luckily, Chrissy felt she owed Grace a favor for the extra business she brought her, so she was willing to oblige.

Once that was resolved, Grace discovered that 'someone' had tampered with her tarts, and there were now little slices of tomato and onion mixed in with the fruit she had so carefully cut up and arranged. The rest of the food had looked untouched, but Grace was no longer confident in what she was serving. So instead of spending the night with Cole, Grace stayed up half the night, remaking all the food she had cooked earlier that day. At this point, she was rooting for Journee and whatever revenge plot she was cooking up.

Too tired to clean up the night before, the kitchen was still a mess when Grace returned to make breakfast. Before long, she found herself slamming doors and loudly tossing utensils around as tears flowed down her cheeks. She jumped and spun around when she felt a hand on her shoulder, ready to attack. Seeing it was Granny, Grace threw her arms around Granny's neck and cried.

"There, there," she said, patting Grace on the back. "What's the cause of all these tears?"

Grace hiccuped as she tried to respond through her sobs. "Everything," she said.

"Everything? That can't be true, can it?"

"I guess not," Grace sobbed. "It just feels like everything."

"This day has always been hard for you, my dear. It's okay to take some time to process your feelings."

"I haven't had time for that," Grace let go and reached for a paper towel to blow her nose. "Besides that, it's just been so crazy around here."

"Maybe next year we should skip this holiday," Granny said wisely. "You need more time between these

'Experiences' of yours. They seem to be taking a toll on you."

Grace nodded in agreement. "I've just felt so tired lately. Physically and emotionally."

"How about we take a couple of months off? No major holidays are coming up, and you can take some time to see if you want to keep doing this."

"Of course I need to keep doing this," Grace exclaimed.

"I said 'want,' my dear. There is a difference. Things have changed a lot around here over the last several months. It might be time to reevaluate."

"At the very least, I'm willing to agree to take some time off." She took a deep breath to calm her nerves and let it out slowly. "I just need to get through the rest of this day."

"I'll be right here by your side the whole time," Granny reassured her. "If you need anything, just let me know."

Grace wrapped her arms around Granny once more. "Thanks, Granny. You're the best."

Granny looked around the kitchen. "Now, what can I do to help?"

"You can go sit down," Grace said with a laugh. "You're not supposed to spend much time on your feet, remember?"

"I'm feeling pretty good right now, but you're right. I will need to keep my strength up if I'm going to make it through the day. I can chop, though," she raised her brow in question.

"That would be helpful. I'm making stuffed French toast again and would like to put some strawberries on top."

"Perfect! I'll sit at the bar, and we can talk while we work."

Grace filled Granny in on all the gossip going around town, Granny filling in some gaps courtesy of Gladys and her never-ending network of local spies. By the time breakfast was ready, they were laughing so hard that Grace once again had tears rolling down her cheeks. Despite everything, she could not have asked for a better start to the day.

***

The table was set with the fancy tablecloth, the 'good' china, and the real silverware. Two goblets were in front of each plate, one for water and one for wine, and there were two beautiful floral centerpieces made of white carnations for the finishing touch. She wasn't one to brag, but Grace felt it looked magazine-worthy and hoped her guests were just as impressed.

After several taste tests, just to be sure, Grace felt confident the new food she had spent half the night making was tamper-free, so she put it on the bar for guests to help themselves. Cole and Riley were set to arrive at any minute and would be responsible for grilling the steaks she had been marinating since she bought them two days before.

While they waited for the guys to show up, Grace gathered everyone in the living room so she could hand out their presents. Each guest, including Molly, Granny, and

Gladys, received a bouquet of pink and white carnations and a gift bag containing the framed photograph. In addition, Grace had convinced Grant to give her a copy of Molly's ultrasound for her picture frame, and Granny and Gladys's held photos of Grace's favorite memories with them.

"Oh my gosh," Molly exclaimed when she opened her bag. "I can't believe you did this for me; thank you so much." There were tears in her eyes when she stood up to hug Grace, and dang it, Grace felt tears stinging the back of hers as well.

Gladys and Granny were showing each other their pictures, and even from her place across the room, Grace could see that they were reminiscing. The rest of the duos were happily chatting, which left Rebekah. Since Amelia had spent most of her short time there alone, and Grace didn't think Rebekah wanted a reminder of her time with Amelia anyway, Grace had put a picture of herself and Rebekah in the frame. It was a picture she had taken of them out at the ranch one morning. They were dirty, smelly, and sweaty, but they were laughing, and for the first time since Grace had met her, Rebekah looked happy.

"Thank you," she said, holding the picture frame to her chest. "I'll treasure it always."

Unsure of how to take that, Grace smiled and turned her attention to the rest of the group. Did she hate the photo? Was it too cheeky of her to assume that Rebekah would want a picture of the two of them? Or was she, too, missing her mother and feeling the sting of the holiday? Grace should have given more thought to the fact that, in a way, Rebekah had just lost her mother. This day had to be painful, more so since she was surrounded by a group of happy mother/daughter duos.

"Can I have everyone's attention?" Valerie called out to the room.

It took a moment for the chatter to die down, several guests rolling their eyes while others seemed to brace themselves for Valerie's next dramatic display.

"While it's so sweet and thoughtful of Grace to do this," she said sarcastically, "I want to show you what the real Grace is like." She pulled out a laptop and set it on a table where everyone could see. "You know Grace as your goody-two-shoes hostess. I know her for the husband-stealing, loud-mouthed, slimy snake she is. And I'm going to show you proof."

"You just can't help yourself, can you, Valerie," Cole said from the doorway. He looked at the woman claiming to be his mother. "Hello, Brenda, haven't seen you in, oh, eight years, give or take."

Brenda went white as a sheet at the sight of Cole. She opened her mouth to speak, but nothing came out.

"Who's Brenda?" asked Journee, looking around the room. "Do you mean Anita?"

"No, I mean Brenda. She's Valerie's mother," Cole said, pointing to the woman. "Takes a lot of nerve to use my mom like that," he spat. "She was nothing but kind to you, to both of you, and this is how you repay her? By using her name to torment my girlfriend. You should be ashamed of yourselves."

Brenda hung her head in shame. "I'm sorry, Cole. I never should have agreed to this, but," she shrugged, "she's my daughter. I never have been able to say no to her."

"That actually explains a lot," said Journee.

"Anyway," Valerie waved them off as if they were nothing more than an annoying gnat buzzing around her head. "It's time to watch the video. You too, Cole. You're going to want to see this."

Valerie pressed play, but nothing happened. Confused, she checked the video files and then tried again, to no avail. Now visibly frustrated, she bashed the play button repeatedly, then gave up and screamed. "This can't be happening!" She stomped her heels and threw herself on the ground in full tantrum mode.

The entire room watched in shock as Valerie regressed to a two-year-old having a meltdown over being forced to wear socks. This continued for several minutes before Cole shook his head and looked at Grace. "Are those steaks ready?"

"Yeah," she looked at Valerie one last time. "Let me get them for you."

Most of the guests followed them out of the room, heading to the deck to escape the noise. Journee followed Grace and Cole into the kitchen. "I suppose I'm to blame for that," she said sheepishly.

"What do you mean?" asked Grace.

"I'm the one that erased her video." She lit up with a huge grin when she saw the look on Grace's face. "I overheard her diabolical plan last night, so while everyone was distracted by the gift bags, I reached over and hit the delete button."

"I don't know what to say," said Grace. Her eyes filled with tears for the umpteenth time that day. "Thank you doesn't seem good enough."

"Nah, I was happy to do it. You didn't deserve to be slandered like that. Especially after you have been so kind to all of us."

"Thank you," Cole offered his hand for her to shake. "It's too bad you're leaving tomorrow; we sure could use you around here."

"I doubt she'll be around for long now that her plan backfired. I'm going to find my mom. Thanks for the photo, Grace. This has been one of the best vacations I've taken with my mom, and I'll treasure that memory forever."

Grace nodded in response, too choked up to speak. When Journee was out of sight, Grace threw herself into Cole's arms and hung on for dear life.

"Are you okay?" he asked, concern in his voice.

She nodded against his chest, though she felt she was anything but. Even though Journee had thwarted Valerie's plan, Grace still felt humiliated. She would give just about anything to have the freedom to run to her room and hide under the covers until the guests left the following day.

"Oh look, another sickening display of weakness from the man-stealing loser," Valerie snarked.

Cole's arms tightened around Grace, preventing her from turning around to face her enemy. "What is it you really want, Valerie? And for the first time in your life, please tell the truth," Cole replied.

"She's broke," said Brenda. "And desperate. Her boyfriend kicked her out after discovering she was faking a pregnancy. So she has nowhere to go and no money to support herself."

"Why can't she stay with you?" asked Grace. Since she was still pressed against Cole's chest, her words came out muffled.

"I retired to a one-bedroom condo down in Florida a few years ago," Brenda explained.

"Aren't you a little young for that?" asked Cole.

"Maybe a little," she laughed. "But there's a lot of eligible bachelors down there. I have a never-ending supply of men willing to take me out to dinner right outside my doorstep."

"That sounds like a perfect place for Valerie," came Grace's muffled reply. Cole relaxed his arms enough that she could turn to face the woman while remaining safe in his embrace.

"Those men are too old," Valerie wrinkled her nose in disgust. "I may be desperate, but I'm not that desperate."

"Anyway, I believe my daughter has caused enough problems," she turned to face Valerie. "It's time for me to go, and you're coming with me."

"I'm not going anywhere with you," Valerie shouted.

"You don't have to leave with her, but you can't stay here," Grace informed her.

"We're paid up through tomorrow morning, remember?"

"Actually, Anita Reed is paid up through tomorrow morning. I don't have a reservation for Valerie Thornton, so technically, you're trespassing."

"Whatever, I'm tired of looking at your stupid face anyway," she stomped past her mom and up the stairs, grumbling the whole way.

"I'll make sure she doesn't do anything to that pretty room you put us in," Brenda assured her. "I'm sorry for my part in this and for impersonating your mother, Cole."

"I appreciate that, Brenda. I hope the next time we meet, it's on better terms."

Brenda nodded and moved toward the stairs, stopping when she reached the doorway. "I wish it would have worked out between you and my daughter; take care of him," she said to Grace.

"Is it finally over?" Grace whispered. She buried her face in his chest and breathed in deeply, his scent calming her nerves.

"Hopefully," he said into her hair. "As much as I like holding you, we've got a group of hungry people outside. I better get those steaks on."

She reluctantly let go, pulled the steaks out of the fridge, and handed them to him. They walked outside together and were greeted by cheers when the guests saw the steaks in his hand. While Cole fired up the grill, Grace did her best to mingle with the guests, but her heart wasn't in it. Thankfully, Molly and Rebekah did a great job covering for her while she excused herself to the kitchen for some last-minute pre-dinner prep work.

Now that Valerie was gone, the rest of the day went off without a hitch, the guests seeming to enjoy themselves once the drama died down. When it was finally over, she dragged herself upstairs and plopped down on her bed, thoroughly exhausted. She had just completed another successful Experience. It was time for a break, and she had more than earned it.

The Day After

G race had been so exhausted the night before, she had slept through her alarm clock. She would probably still be asleep if Rebekah hadn't come in to wake her. Too tired to care how she looked, she went to the ranch in the clothes she had slept in. Rebekah had attempted to make small talk, but Grace had spaced out and inadvertently ignored her.

When they arrived at the ranch, Cole stood outside talking to Officer Smith. "What's going on?" Grace asked in concern.

"Someone stole my RV," replied Cole.

"That old thing you had sitting by the barn?"

"Yeah, that's the one."

"Why would anyone want to steal that? Does it even run?"

"That's just it; it starts but needs a new engine. Whoever stole it will be lucky to make it a hundred miles before it ends up dead on the side of the road. Going to be really inconvenient if they're stuck between towns."

Grace shook her head in disbelief. "Did they take anything else?"

"Not that I can tell. Honestly, I wouldn't have even bothered Officer Smith if it weren't for the liability issue. That thing is practically worthless."

"Okay, well, I need to get moving so I can get back in time to make breakfast before everyone leaves. Nice to see you again, Officer."

Rebekah followed Grace over to the barn. "What's the deal with the cop back there?"

"What do you mean?"

"He seemed embarrassed."

"Last time I saw him, he arrested an eighty-year-old woman for harassing me and a few others. We'd had a few run-ins before that and didn't end on very good terms."

"He's cute," Rebekah stated.

Grace looked at her over the top of her sunglasses. "I guess. If you like the Andy Griffith type."

"Who's Andy Griffith?"

"Never mind," Grace sighed. Rebekah had obviously not spent her youth watching re-runs on Nick at Nite with her Granny like Grace had. "Anyway, I thought you were interested in Riley."

Rebekah shrugged. "That doesn't mean a girl can't look. Besides, he still hasn't asked me out on a second date."

"Did you tell him that you plan to stay?"

"It hasn't come up yet..." she trailed off.

"Oh? Does that mean you changed your mind? And if so, about him or staying?"

They took turns dumping the contents of their shovels into the wagon. It was still cool out, but not enough to keep the sweat from dripping down their backs. "Not about staying," she said quickly. "But maybe about Riley. I overheard him talking to Grant about Katie, and I guess I just lost interest. I've never had a boyfriend that was interested in me for me. So it might be nice to have someone who looks at me like Cole looks at you for a change."

"That could still be Riley," said Grace. "If the only issue was him thinking you're leaving today, you could easily fix that."

"Yeah, but he never asked even once. Shouldn't that have been his first question if he was interested?"

Grace couldn't argue with that logic, though the matchmaker in her desperately wanted to. "Fine, I'm still not convinced Officer Smith should be next in line."

"Cole seems to like him," Rebekah pointed out.

"Maybe," Grace replied hesitantly.

"I wouldn't worry about it; I'm more concerned about my financial future than my romantic one."

"Any news on that front?"

"Actually, yes. I've been meaning to ask you if I can borrow your car this afternoon. The couple from the winery called, and they wanted to meet with me to discuss a partnership. I might get my first real client!" she said excitedly.

Grace stood up straight and leaned against her shovel. "That's great!" she exclaimed. "And, of course, you can borrow my car. So what kind of partnership are you talking about?"

"I posted some pictures of their winery on my socials, and apparently, they've been getting a lot of interest from potential customers. They want to discuss hiring me to do some promotions for them. Paid promotions!"

"I'm confused. Isn't that something you were already doing?"

"Yes, but it feels different now. Those brands wanted to work with Rebekah, the socialite; From Vines to Wines wants to work with the new and improved Rebekah."

"Hmm," Grace said thoughtfully. "If Wyatt and Kenzie want to work with you because you're bringing the big city here, what if you worked with big city brands to bring their products to the country?"

"I'm not sure I follow," she stated.

"Two words: country chic," Grace held up her fingers for emphasis.

"Hasn't that already been done?"

"To a point, but not by someone like you. We could take pictures of you wearing some name-brand outfit in front of the ranch. You could talk about your date with the sexy cowboy while wearing boots or something. Heck, you could even decorate your room with décor from some fancy department. People would eat that stuff up."

"You know, you might be on to something. I'll talk it over with Molly and see what she says."

Grace was a little offended by that but held her tongue. Molly was the expert on all things marketing, while Grace still hadn't gotten around to opening a single social media account. Oh well, there were some benefits to being out of the loop. She would be the least likely to get the blame if something went wrong.

They finished up and headed for the car, no sign of Cole, Officer Smith, or Riley. "It'll be nice to have the house to ourselves again," Grace commented.

"I hate to say it, but I might actually miss Valerie. She was a huge pain, but she kept things entertaining."

"At my expense!" Grace exclaimed.

"And Journee's," Rebekah laughed. "The way those two went at each other, you'd think they were life-long enemies or something."

"True. Although, I, for one, will not miss any of it. This was the most stressed out I've ever been, and I spent last Easter harassed by an angry mob of elderly protesters."

"I'm sorry I wasn't here to witness that. The way Granny and Gladys talked, it sounded pretty hilarious."

"It wasn't at the time," Grace muttered.

***

Just as they'd arrived together, the guests decided to leave together. Grace followed them onto the porch to say goodbye and exchanged hugs and well wishes. A small part of her was sad to see them go.

As they walked to their cars, Kate pulled her aside. "I don't know what you said to Izzie the other day, but I am forever in your debt. After your conversation, her attitude did a complete eighty, and we've been getting along ever since. In fact, we're already planning our next mother/daughter vacation for later this summer!"

"I'm delighted to hear that," Grace replied. "Just don't..."

"Squander it?" Kate laughed. "Trust me; I have no intention to." She started toward the steps, stopped, and turned back around. "Hey, make sure you keep us on your email list. We might want to do this again sometime."

Grace nodded and waved goodbye one last time. Did they have an email list? She would have to ask Molly. They should consider starting one if they haven't already. Grace could think of several guests she would love to see again. With that in mind, she turned to go back inside, only to see Cole standing in the doorway. She was so startled to see him that she let out a yelp and jumped back, managing to catch herself just before she fell backward down the front steps.

"Whoa," he said, reaching out to steady her. "Didn't mean to scare you like that, darlin'. Are you okay?"

"I'm fine," she replied, breathing heavily. "I just didn't expect to see you there. Aren't you supposed to be working?"

Cole grinned. "I thought you'd be at least a little excited to see me," he teased.

She swatted his arm and rolled her eyes. "Of course, I'm thrilled to see you, silly. I can't remember the last time I saw you at this time of day."

"It really wasn't that long ago; it just feels that way. So anyway, I have decided to take the day off to spend it with you." He pulled her into his arms and kissed her. "And don't ask me if I have time for this," he said when he pulled back and saw the expression on her face. "I've decided to make time."

A dreamy expression crossed her face as she smiled up at him. "Is there anything, in particular, you would like to do on our day off?"

"There are many things I would like to do," he said huskily. "But our day is already planned."

"Oh," Grace raised her brow. "What are we doing?"

"We're going to start with a massage over at A Gentle Touch; then we're going to go see Lula at Lulu's, followed by an appointment at Chrissy's where you will choose a new outfit to wear to our private dinner date out on the back deck this evening."

Tears pooled in the back of her eyes. "You planned a spa day for me?"

"I had a little help," he admitted. "You do so much for everyone else; I think it's time we do something for you."

"Thank you," she hugged him close as the tears threatened to spill. "Wait a minute," she pulled back to look at him. "You said we're having dinner on the deck. Who's doing that?"

"Rebekah has volunteered to be our chef for the evening."

"Oh no," Grace groaned.

"I heard that," Rebekah joked as she joined them on the porch. "Don't worry, I have everything under control," she continued into the house.

"There's frozen pizza in the freezer out in the garage," Grace called after her.

"Oh, thank goodness," she muttered just loud enough for them to hear.

Grace laughed as she turned back to Cole. "Sounds like a perfect day. When do we start?"

Cole looked at his watch. "We're supposed to meet Amy in about an hour. There are a few things I need to 'take care of' out at the ranch in the meantime. Mind tagging along?"

"Not at all," she said, hoping she was not misinterpreting his meaning. They walked hand-in-hand down the steps and over to his truck. "What about Riley?"

"Um," he hesitated to answer. "He's spending the day with Katie."

"Oh," she hopped into the truck and slid over to the middle seat, wanting to stay as close to him as possible. Time was precious, and she was determined to make the most of every second they had together. "I guess it didn't matter she decided to stay?" she asked when he got in on the driver's side.

"I guess not, but there are plenty of other available men—" he stopped when he saw the look of doubt on her face.

They drove in silence for a couple of minutes, Grace absentmindedly playing with the hair at the nape of his neck. "I did hear that a new doctor is moving to town. Maybe he'll be single."

"If we're thinking of the same guy, he's a veterinarian, not a human doctor. From what I've heard, coming here is a bit of a punishment for him. So...."

"What happened to Hailey?" Grace hated to lose the woman who had become something of a friend ever since she helped them out with Ruby and her puppies last Christmas.

"Hailey's husband got a job offer he couldn't refuse in a town up north, so Hailey is going with him. Losing her is going to be a real blow to the farming community. We have always been able to count on her, day or night. Unfortunately, this new guy does not sound like the type to appreciate making house calls at three in the morning."

"Hopefully, the rumors will turn out to be false this time."

"Don't be surprised if he ends up on your doorstep. He hasn't had time to buy a house, and there are zero rentals in town. You've developed a reputation as the go-to place for transitional housing."

The house came into view, a welcome respite from the usual chaos. "I guess we'll see how it goes. In the meantime..." she followed him out of the truck and raced him inside, laughing when he let her win only to grab her from behind and throw her over his shoulder. From the looks of things, she had not misinterpreted his meaning.

No one knows what the future holds. All you can do is treasure the time you have with the people you love. At the end of the day, that's what really matters.

Afterword

Dear Reader,

Thank you so much for reading *Countdown to Mother's Day*. I hope you enjoyed reading it as much as I enjoyed writing it! As an author of books with a revolving cast of characters, some of them tend to stand out more than others, and Rebekah Rutherford was one of those characters. Despite my attempts to leave her in the past, she kept popping up and demanding I redeem her character, as she insisted that I needlessly slandered her!

I have no idea if we'll hear from Hunter or Amelia again, but it seems likely we will at least get an update from time to time. As for Valerie, there was just too much material to cover in one book, so Valerie will be getting her own series! I love a good redemption arc, and while I think hers will take a little longer than Rebekah's, I have hope for her. Look for her new book: *Hope Bloom in Willow Glen*.

If you enjoyed this book, it would be awesome if you would leave a review. As an indie author, reviews help so much in bringing new readers to my books. Also, if you would like to join my newsletter, you can do so at diannahouxshop.com.

As always, I would love to hear from you, so feel free to send an email with your thoughts.

Happy Reading!

—Dianna Houx

About the Author

Hi! I'm a small-town girl who never outgrew her love for heartfelt stories and happily-ever-afters. I live in a rural Missouri town of twenty-five hundred people with my husband and three boys in a late 1800s home we're lovingly restoring—one project (and paintstroke) at a time.

When I'm not writing, I enjoy reading, perusing antique stores, or dreaming up my next story on the porch swing with glass of lemonade in hand!

My stories are seasoned with over-the-top, funny happenings in small-town settings, but at their heart, they're about real people with relatable struggles, hopes, and dreams. I write to entertain—and to remind readers that even the wildest moments can lead to something beautiful.

Learn more at diannahouxshop.com.

www.ingramcontent.com/pod-product-compliance
Lightning Source LLC
Chambersburg PA
CBHW022102050726
47591CB00002B/633